A DARLING HANDYMAN

DARLING MEN
BOOK ONE

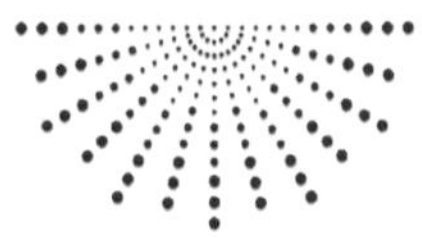

LARK HOLIDAY

GLASS ELEPHANT PRESS

To Papa, who was here when I started this story. I'm glad it took this long to write. I'm glad that there were so many days I skipped writing so we could go for a long drive instead. Even if I was slightly terrified by your driving at times. Even if we had nowhere to go. I'm glad we wasted so much time. My only regret is not wasting more.

PROLOGUE

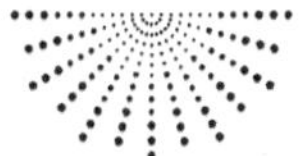

Natasha Owens awoke with a start. Sitka spruce trees tapped on the thin glass of the trailer window as she held her mother's quilt to her chin and blinked into the night. The last bit of winter held on with a chill in the air.

A sliver of moonlight found its way through the trees and cut across the inside of the trailer, teasing a glimpse of Natasha's life. The handle of a glass tea cup. The title of a romance book. The wooden tray where her wedding ring sat.

Once in a while, Natasha would try the ring on. But whereas it had once felt like part of her body, it was now heavy and unfamiliar. Whenever she picked it up, a perfect circle sat in the dust.

She'd spent years as a widow. Not that people called her that. It was too simple a term to describe how they felt about her, a bizarre old lady who lived alone in the forest and saw glimpses of the future.

Natasha didn't see the stares as much as she felt them. As if she wouldn't—she had the sight after all. Though most of the locals doubted her. Only when people needed her sight, did they believe in it with all their hearts. Desperation could make a person cling to any scrap of hope, much in the same way winter refused to release its hold on this island.

Natasha sighed, staring into the dark. Wind whistled through the treetops, and a few stray pine needles landed on the roof, as lightly as the steps of a cat's paw.

She wouldn't be able to sleep tonight, that was the curse of the sight. She didn't choose when it happened, or even what it would be about. Sometimes the sight faded away for so long she doubted she had it at all. But it always returned, bright and snapping, calling for her.

Natasha rose from the bed and grabbed an afghan to wrap around her shoulders. She flicked on a light, suddenly feeling vulnerable alone in the dark. The lit room was a glowing beacon in the forest, but then again, who was here to see?

Sitting down at the small formica tabletop, she shuffled her cards, the worn edges tugging at her heart—her mother had given her these cards.

"The most important thing is to tell the truth," her mom had told her, caressing the side of Natasha's face.

Natasha reached up to touch her cheek now, the skin looser and more wrinkled than in that memory. She was certain no one felt old in their hearts, but she did feel her age when the cold of winter sucked the life from her body and made her bones ache.

She knew she needed to find a home besides this old trailer, but knowing she needed something didn't magically make it a possibility. This island was a place without options.

She laid out the cards, noting each image. Her dream she'd awakened from was still at the forefront of her mind, and Natasha knew she was fooling herself. She didn't need the cards, not really. And yet, they were the only tool she had to reassure herself. It wasn't like she could ask anyone else.

There was nowhere and no one in town for her. The place was folding, collapsing on itself like a dying star.

When Natasha had first seen Darling all those years ago, it had been love at first sight. Cheerful buildings had sat in a row like Fabergé eggs. Everyone had been excited to meet the wife of Charles Owens, the direct descendant of the town's founder. His bloodline had even been a maternal line, and for that Natasha had thought it stronger.

Those first few years had been as if blessed by God. Charles had been happy to steal her away from Sitka, and he'd built her a beautiful home here. But that was then. Now she was one of the few left—tragedy or temptation having lured the others away one by one.

"You don't end up here by accident," Charles had said on a day when they'd sailed out to sea and were gazing back at the shoreline. "You have to want it."

Natasha had wanted nothing more than Charles and, of course, children. They'd had twins, a boy and a girl, and the day they were born had been the happiest day of her life.

She'd thought the saddest would be when Charles had left this earth.

She had been wrong.

Natasha closed her eyes, trapping a tear.

But her vision had not been about Charles.

She turned over the card she had been waiting for. Death stared back at her.

Natasha knew as well as anyone that humans assigned meaning to everything, good or bad, to suit their agenda. This was the danger of sharing with others what was to come. What she saw had already happened, yet people believed they could change it.

She had seen the way the locals who had sought her out for guidance held their breath when she flipped over the Death card, as if their days were numbered. But it almost never meant that. Not in her experience. More often than not, it meant a new beginning.

So Natasha gave no feelings to what she had seen. She only knew two things for sure. *Andre was dead. And Sarah was coming back to Darling.* Change would be there soon. Both hellos and goodbyes.

A narrow yellow beam came through the window as the sun reached out to warm the treetops—tomorrow was here.

Natasha flicked off the light, keeping the afghan around her shoulders as she climbed back into bed.

"A new day for Darling," she whispered, as her eyes fluttered closed.

CHAPTER ONE

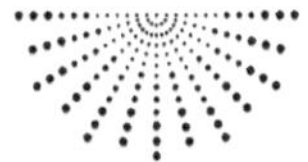

Sarah Carter hated when she proved herself right. She should've stuck to her no dating at work policy. Then she wouldn't be late to work with a hangover from hell. She fought the temptation to bang her head against the wall and ask herself why she'd done it. But Sarah had been begging life for answers for the past five years, and it hadn't done any good. After all, it wasn't as if answers would change what had happened.

The morning was on a definite downward trajectory. After inching along in LA traffic, suffering a throbbing headache, and praying her boss didn't notice she was late, Sarah finally arrived at the coffee shop. There was just one problem—the woman standing at the counter was trying to kill her.

That was the only plausible explanation as to why the perky blonde in yoga pants was ordering the entire right side of the menu. There was no way she would actually eat all that. Based on her tiny waist and unblemished skin, the woman probably subsisted on three organic almonds and a glass of sparkling water a day. She looked like almost everyone else in Los Angeles—pretty plastic people, too perfect for problems.

Sarah tapped her fingers against her thigh. Every minute felt like a lifetime. She had a million things to do at the office, and she hadn't planned on spending twenty minutes waiting to get a black coffee and something to eat.

She shifted to her other foot, trying to remember the breathing exercises she'd read about in that magazine. She forced her breath out, feeling light-headed after two rounds. Maybe she wasn't getting it right. The exercise was supposed to calm her down, not render her unconscious.

Her phone rang, and Sarah clenched her jaw. She couldn't remember the last time she'd actually turned her phone off. But time was money, and work never stopped.

She hadn't grown up dreaming of being a headhunter. Then again, she hadn't had an inkling that she would end up in Los Angeles either. Competition in the industry was fierce, but Sarah had something most people didn't; a complete lack of a personal life. She gave every free minute, every spare ounce of energy, and all her brain power to the job.

Sarah reached for her cell phone and winced when she saw the caller ID. Even worse than work—it was her parents. This was the fifth time they'd called this week. Like the other four times, Sarah didn't answer. She told herself she would answer their tenth phone call. Hopefully that would buy her a few more days.

She didn't have the energy for that conversation right now. Even thinking about it made her shoulders slump forward with exhaustion. Her parents always wanted to know the same thing: When was she coming home?

No matter how many times Sarah told them she was

never coming back, they didn't stop asking. It was like watching someone get in an elevator and push the button over and over again, convinced that maybe this time it would go side-to-side instead of up and down. Like the elevator, Sarah wasn't built that way.

Her phone went silent, and her stomach twisted with guilt. Her parents were the ones who'd made sure she had had enough cash to get a place to live the minute she'd gotten to Los Angeles. Sarah had been hysterical, desperate to leave everything behind. If it hadn't been for her parents, she would've been living on the street. She knew they loved her. But avoiding home had nothing to do with her parents. They didn't understand. Sarah could never go back, not after what she had done.

Finally, the woman at the counter stepped away, and the rest of the line lurched forward like caffeine-deprived zombies.

Sarah placed her order and, in less than ten minutes, walked out with her coffee in hand. She blinked into the sunlight that reached through the smoggy sky. Her vision blurred for a minute before she could pull down her sunglasses. Sarah hadn't slept more than four hours a night for the past couple of months.

She needed a break. But rest came with time to think, and that was something Sarah strictly avoided. Because no matter how often she wondered why everything had happened like it did back in Alaska, she never seemed to have an answer.

* * *

SARAH PUSHED BACK the double glass doors, shivering as she walked through a blast of cold air. The sweat disappeared from her forehead. Heat this early in the year promised a long, hot summer. Sarah dreaded the stifling weather already.

She dipped her chin as she passed the security guard in the lobby. The man in uniform didn't give her a second glance. For the last several years, Sarah had been the first one in this building every morning. The security guards had ceased to notice her, as if she had become part of the building itself. She could be a decorative fiddle-leaf fig for all they cared. It wasn't like back home, where everyone was in her business.

Sarah hit the button on the elevator before forcing herself to turn around and take the stairs. Her job didn't leave a lot of time for the gym, so taking the stairs was the extent of her daily exercise.

Gasping as she reached the sixth floor, she was thankful no one else was there yet. Everyone in this town was a fitness model. She didn't need a judgmental look to know she was not. But Sarah didn't care about fitting in. After growing up in a small town where nothing went unnoticed, she only cared about blending in.

Just as Sarah closed her office door behind her, a trill came from her purse. With a choice word, Sarah set her to-go order down on her desk and reached for the phone. A quick glance at the caller ID told her she couldn't ignore it.

Her boss, Desirae, didn't waste time on chit chat. "Look, I know it's Friday night, but I have a potential client for you who wants to meet as soon as possible. Tell me you don't have plans."

Sarah's shoulders drooped as she thought about the bottle of chardonnay chilling in her fridge. "I don't have plans. Let me grab a pen—"

"No need," Desirae interrupted. "I'll send you an email with everything. I have you booked in for Monet's tonight."

Sarah crossed her arms. It wasn't her boss's fault that she

assumed Sarah would drop everything for work, it was Sarah's for doing exactly that every time Desirae asked.

"Monet's sounds great." At least that part was true. The restaurant was one of the best in the city.

Desirae let out a sigh. "Thank you. Trust me, this guy is worth big money."

Sarah ended the call and reached for her coffee. As she leaned back in her chair, she gazed out the floor-to-ceiling windows at the city skyline. Sarah knew she needed to stop taking last-minute work meetings. She should be out there, trying to have a life that went beyond a single date. But work kept her busy, too busy and too tired, to get attached to anyone. Sarah liked it that way.

That's a sign of PTSD, keeping busy all the time, her brother had told her.

As if that was news to her. Of course, she had PTSD. She had lost everything. Her brother, in his perfect little world, thought life was so simple. He didn't know what had really happened. No one did.

The sun shone down over the city. Sarah could see the faint reflection of her face in the window, floating over Los Angeles. This was where she belonged now. This was where she would stay.

Her stomach growled, and she turned back to her desk. She opened her laptop and reached for her food. Sarah took a bite of her breakfast sandwich and groaned. It was cold.

It was going to be one of those days.

* * *

Peering in the visor mirror, Sarah touched up her lipstick and brushed a few errant strands of hair out of her face. She had pulled out all the stops for tonight's meeting. She was even wearing her nice heels, the ones that made her feet hurt after just two hours.

When Sarah was certain everything was in place, she opened her car door to hand off her keys to the valet.

A chime came from her clutch. Sarah pulled out her phone to silence it when she saw Aaron's name. Her stomach twisted up. He'd texted when she'd gotten home from work, asking when he would see her again. Sarah had told him tonight was off the table and sent him a picture of her all done up.

Sometimes she really hated herself. She needed to end things, not lead him on. Sarah had no plans to ever be in a relationship again, much less with a former client.

Smoothing out her dress, she took a deep breath and headed through the heavy double doors.

This client must be a big deal, or Desirae wouldn't have called in whatever favor it took to get a last-minute reservation at Monet's.

Sarah breezed into the restaurant like a celebrity on the red carpet.

Fake it till you make it.

Except she had been faking it for so long, she wasn't sure what was real anymore.

Sarah smiled at the hostess. "Reservation for Carter."

The willowy blonde scanned her computer. "Right this way. Mr. Carter has already arrived."

Sarah frowned. That didn't make sense. The lack of sleep must finally be catching up to her. "My name is Carter."

The hostess blinked at her, her eyelashes fanning like palm fronds. "Right," she said in a voice that made it clear she didn't care. Then she stepped out from the podium and led Sarah past the lobby into the belly of the restaurant.

They passed by men in suits and women in couture. Servers presented bottles of wine older than Sarah and ground fresh pepper over filet mignon. The atmosphere was exclusive, luxurious, and everything Alaska was not. She had wanted to get as far away as possible from everything that reminded her of home, and she couldn't have picked a better place.

The hostess gestured with her hand. "Your table."

Sarah's face fell. Her mouth was dry, and her words stuck in her throat.

The man smiled and pulled out a chair for her. "Ms. Carter, so lovely to meet with you. Thank you for accepting the last minute invitation."

The hostess faded into the background, leaving just the two of them.

He cracked the menu open. "What are you in the mood to drink? I think I am going to order something strong."

"Mac," Sarah spat out, finally gathering her wits. "What the hell are you doing here?"

CHAPTER TWO

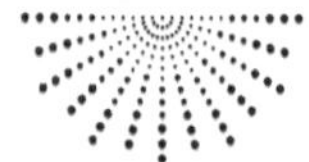

SARAH

His smile was cold—a predator baring his teeth. "What's wrong? You aren't happy to see me, little sister?"

Sarah felt light-headed. Maverick Carter here in Los Angeles. It wasn't possible. As far as her brother was concerned, the map ended at the Alaska state line. "I'm experiencing a lot of emotions right now. I'm not sure happiness is one of them, but I'll keep you posted."

She reached for her water, the ice cubes clinking as she raised the glass to her lips. Sarah stilled her hand—like an animal her brother could sense fear.

The server came, and Mac ordered whiskey for both of them.

"I don't drink whiskey anymore," Sarah said.

Mac raised his hands in the air. "Sorry, lady. I don't really know you anymore, seeing as you don't visit or call."

She clenched her teeth. It had taken all of five minutes for Mac to give her crap. She shouldn't be surprised. He'd never had much compassion for her. "I talked to Mom and Dad on the phone last week."

He barked a laugh. "Briefly. And refused their invitation to come home, just like I told them you would."

She leaned forward, looking him in the eye. "Do they know you're here?"

Mac snorted. "Are you kidding? No way. Nothing can upset the balance with their precious little girl. But here's the difference between them and me: I don't have the patience for your bullshit."

He accepted his drink from the server, baring his teeth again.

Sarah took a gulp of her own drink, savoring the burn. Maybe she did like whiskey. Or maybe that was the panic talking. "Here I thought you were just the brute force of the family. I bet you're feeling pretty smart, coming up with this plan to schedule a work meeting with me."

Mac lifted a shoulder. "You always go hunting for prey in its natural habitat."

She gestured to the restaurant. "Unfortunately, you're going back empty-handed. You said it yourself. This is my natural habitat now."

He rolled his eyes. "There is no way in hell you can be happy here. I feel ready for antidepressants, and I only just landed. I am going to spell this out for you. You're going back. Even if I have to carry you."

Sarah set her jaw. If she wasn't so upset with him right now, she might be impressed. Mac had come all the way here, faked being a client, and even changed out of jeans for once. "Give me one good reason."

"I'll give you three." Mac held up one finger. "You don't answer your phone more than half the time." A second finger came up. "If you do, you keep the conversations as short as the patience of an angry man." The third finger. "Three.

Mom fell and hurt herself, you jackass. They had to shut the lodge down, and they were hoping you could help."

Sarah's stomach sank. "Why didn't they tell me?"

Mac looked at her like she was stupid. "Can I bring your attention back to points one and two? You talked to them, remember? Tell me how that went."

Sarah swallowed. She had been annoyed, tired of her parents asking her to come home. "They didn't tell me anything. They just asked me when I was coming back."

Mac threw back the rest of his whiskey and signaled to the server for another. "God forbid they ever inconvenience their perfect daughter. That's why I am telling you now. You need to go back. It's time."

Sarah stared into her glass, trying to focus on anything but the pit of dread in her stomach. Mac had no idea what he was asking of her. "I can't go back."

"Won't. You won't go back there. There is a difference."

Sarah's chest grew tight. She didn't give a damn about the difference. She was never stepping foot in Alaska again. "It doesn't matter. Besides, I'm really busy with work."

"And mom just got hurt. Stop being selfish." His voice grew quiet, causing a chill to travel down Sarah's spine. Yelling was Mac's way of communicating. Whispering meant he was pissed.

"Look, kid. You weren't at the last family board meeting, so let me get you up to speed. My flights are the only thing keeping us afloat right now. On a good day, the lodge broke even."

Sarah chewed on her lip. She hadn't known the money situation was that bad. Though her parents weren't rich by any means, they had always made do. But maybe that meant there was a way out of this. "Money? I could give them money. Like I said, I've been working a lot, and I've been saving and—"

Mac's jaw fell open. "Seriously? Wow. You've been away a long time. Their own parents couldn't get them to stay in Connecticut with money. What they want is this lodge. They put their heart and soul into it. I don't understand why you can't get your ass up to Alaska and help your family for a change. Who else are they gonna ask?"

Sarah twisted her hands. The worst part was Mac was right. After her parents, no one knew how to run that place better than her. She had worked at the lodge as long as she could remember, from helping with odd jobs as a kid up to managing the whole thing as an adult. She could handle the housekeeping, meal service, and the making of reservations. It would be impossible to ask the same of anyone else.

She leaned back in her chair and massaged her forehead. Sarah could feel the stares. This restaurant was a place where business deals were made and people got engaged. Not one where you rehashed family drama that created tension so thick you could cut it with one of the German-made steak knives laid out on the table.

Sarah looked away, her throat tight. "It's not a good time."

Mac sighed. "It's never a good time for these things. Never a good time to buy a house. Never a good time to have a baby. Never a good time to fall and get hurt."

Her head pounded. She prayed she didn't throw up right there in the dining room. Her hangover from this morning suddenly seemed pleasant by comparison. "Fine. I'll go."

"Good."

"Good?" she echoed, her blood pressure skyrocketing. "How about saying thank you?"

Mac chuckled. "Yeah, I'm not gonna thank you for being a decent human being. You can leave that hippie crap in California."

Sarah took a deep breath. It shouldn't shock her that her brother was an asshole. What she needed right now was to keep a clear head. "I'm going to need a few days to get everything arranged—"

"Hopefully not more than three," he interrupted. "Because that's when our tickets out of here are for."

Sarah gaped at him. Mac hadn't come here to have a conversation. He had already made the decision for her. "You can't be serious! A two weeks notice. Have you heard of it?"

Mac rolled his eyes. "I hope you haven't been indulging in dope, because your short-term memory has gone to shit. You have a job, remember? The lodge."

Sarah felt another wave of nausea pass over her. She should've never agreed to this. Mac had caught her off guard, which was exactly what he'd wanted. "Okay. Three days."

Mac pushed himself up from the table. "Alright. I'll see you at the airport."

Sarah looked up at him, frowning. "You're leaving?"

Mac snapped his fingers. "Oh, you're right."

He reached for his whiskey. Still standing, he tossed it back right there in the middle of Monet's.

Sarah felt her cheeks heat up as people stared at this strange giant who treated fine dining like a college sports bar.

Before he stepped away, Sarah grabbed his arm. "What did you say, anyway? To Desirae? My boss."

Mac grinned. "I said I was a surgeon. You can be anyone you want online. The Internet is full of tricky shit."

The minute he was out of sight, the server delivered their meals with a flourish. Not that Sarah could eat a single bite right now.

Her stomach sank as she stared at the two perfectly seared ribeyes with sides of garlic mashed potatoes and market greens.

It was ironic, in a way. Once again, Sarah was the one left behind.

Her phone vibrated in her clutch. A text from Aaron telling her he couldn't wait until next week.

Without bothering to reply, Sarah shoved the phone back into her clutch. She didn't care if next week ever came. She wished time would stretch on forever, keeping her from facing the past and all the questions she still didn't have answers to.

* * *

SARAH HAD BEEN RIGHT. It wasn't easy to go back.

Mac had texted her almost hourly—a countdown to when their plane was leaving. She had no doubt he was probably camped outside her condo somewhere with binoculars, just in case she was a flight risk. From anyone else, it would've been psychotic behavior. But that was her brother. If Mac said he was going to do something, he did it. If he intended to get Sarah back to Alaska, then nothing would stop him.

Sarah spent half the morning, and half a bottle of wine, agonizing about what to do with her condo. She finally decided to sublet it. If there was any chance money would fix this situation with her parents, she was going to need every penny.

Her car would have to go, too. Sarah did the math and realized it was cheaper to pay the penalty for breaking her lease early than to hang on to it.

Her stomach churned, a mix of wine and nerves. She still had to figure out what the hell she was going to do about work. With only a few days until their flight left there was no avoiding it. She wondered how much understanding five years of loyalty would get her.

Her hands shook as she tapped on her boss's name.

"I hope you're calling to tell me good news," Desirae said.

Sarah swallowed. "Good news?"

"About the client last night. Did you sign him? I already have a few places in mind. I'll send you an email later."

Sarah paced the floors, the luxury vinyl plank cool against her feet. "Right, the client. No, unfortunately that didn't come through."

"What did you do?"

Sarah's underarms prickled with sweat. She reminded herself that she was the victim here. There was no reason for her to feel guilty. But it was hard to feel any other way after years of practice. "Nothing. I didn't do anything. It wasn't a client. It was my brother. He, um, he has a strong personality. He needed a favor and decided to ask in person."

Desirae let out a whistle. "Must have been one hell of a favor. What did he want? Did he need a surrogate or something?"

Sarah laughed, then immediately slapped her hand over her mouth. The idea of Mac having a kid was as ridiculous as thinking of herself with one.

"I wish." Sarah explained that her mom had gotten hurt and needed Sarah to go back to Alaska for the summer.

"You're not joking," Desirae said.

"No," Sarah answered, uncertain if that was a question or not.

Desirae sighed. "That sucks. I'll miss you. You're my only employee who works as hard as I do."

Sarah's heart rate sped up. "Miss me? I'll be back. This is temporary."

"I get that. But to fill in behind you for the whole summer, that's impossible."

Sarah knew it was true. She had seen her coworkers struggle to take a three-day weekend. Taking months off was unheard of.

Los Angeles was slipping away from her, and she didn't

know if she could start over again. "Please, just think about it."

"I can't make any promises. For now, I'll do my best to keep your job open. You are coming back, right?"

Sarah took a deep breath. She wished Mac had never come here. He'd come to California and invaded her space. He'd interfered with her job, and he'd bought a plane ticket for her without asking.

But Mac had only said he needed Sarah to help while their mom was recovering. He'd said nothing about after their mom was better.

Sarah could buy a plane ticket as easily as he had, right?

"Yes, I'm coming back," Sarah said. "I'm coming back."

"We'll talk then." Desirae ended the call.

Sarah helped herself to the rest of the chardonnay, packing up her suitcase in a booze-infused daze. Even her clothes were a problem. It had been a long time since she'd had to dress for the constant misty rain that fell year round on the Alaskan island where she'd grown up. She did the best she could with what she had and reminded herself that it was all temporary.

* * *

SOMEHOW SHE MADE it to the other side of security at LAX, where she was now waiting to board a flight to a place she had promised herself that she would never go back to.

Temporary.

"Weak as shit." Mac set the paper coffee cup down. He slapped the newspaper he'd been reading down next to it. "Dumb as shit."

Sarah wondered what it was like to be Mac. Everything was black and white to him. Right and wrong. There was no gray space, no room for questions. And who even read newspapers anymore?

Mac folded his hands in his lap and stared straight ahead. He stayed perfectly still, as if he was afraid that California was contagious and it was best not to touch anything. He looked like a lumberjack statue with his flannel shirt and boots.

As she looked at Mac, the airport shrank around Sarah. All the oxygen disappeared, and her chest grew tight as her heart sped up. This was happening. By the end of the day, she would be back in Darling.

Temporary.

She jumped to her feet. "I need a minute."

He turned to look up at her, breaking his perfect form. His eyes narrowed. "Don't go anywhere. This flight leaves in forty-five minutes. We are going to be on that plane."

It wasn't a reminder. It was a threat.

"I don't get why we got here so early in the first place," she hissed. Never in her life had she shown up five hours early for a domestic flight. Not only was her brother grouchy as an old man, but he organized his life like one, too.

"Because I can't wait to get the hell out of here!" Mac yelled as she walked away.

Sarah was certain people were staring, but she was more certain Mac didn't care. He was free from all the rules of real life, and it drove her crazy. The only opinion that mattered was his own.

She struggled to keep her patience as she walked through the busy airport where it seemed the people around her were moving slowly just to annoy her. Sarah kept going until she reached a window overlooking the tarmac at the end of the terminal. Catching a glimpse of the outside instantly soothed her frazzled nerves.

It was so peaceful down there, those tiny people walking

from the tram to the plane. She wondered if her problems would look that small from up here.

Her phone dinged. Another text from Aaron. Sarah checked the time. She had thirty minutes. It was now or never.

Aaron answered after the first ring. "Everything okay?"

Sarah swallowed. "Aaron, there's no easy way to say this. I can't meet up. I have to go home and help my parents. My mom, she's hurt."

"When are you leaving?"

"Today. Right now."

Silence came across the line.

"Aaron?"

"Sorry. I'm just kind of shocked. Of course you have to take care of your mom. Is it serious? What a stupid question, sorry. You wouldn't be going if it wasn't serious."

If only he knew that she was still in shock herself.

"You're fine," Sarah reassured him. "It's bad enough she needs help now, but not forever."

"So you'll be back." She could hear the relief in his voice. "Is there anything I can do to help? Send me the address. I'll have something delivered. Flowers, food, something."

"That's nice of you, really. But it's out of state…"

"Out of state? Which state?"

She rocked back on her heels. Sarah always let people know she was from out of town. She just skipped the detail of exactly how far out of town. "Alaska."

"Alaska," he repeated. "Didn't see that coming."

She cleared her throat. "Aaron, you're great, but—"

"Let me know when you get back, okay? Be safe."

Sarah slipped the phone into her purse. Maybe her feelings about Aaron would change by the time she got back. Maybe she would be happy he hadn't let her make a clean break. But Sarah could still remember what it was like, caring that much about someone. She didn't want to love all the way ever again.

She made her way back to the terminal where Mac sat waiting for her, his face dragged down in a scowl.

"You're cutting it close," he growled.

She held up her hands. "Oh, I'm sorry. I had to rearrange my life. Did that inconvenience you?"

He rolled his eyes. "Here we go with the drama already. Didn't miss that."

Sarah took a deep breath, refusing to get into a battle royale in the middle of domestic departures. "I'm doing what you asked. Coming home while mom gets better."

The flight attendants began checking tickets, and passengers shifted forward. Sarah and Mac grabbed their carry-on bags and crowded around the doorway with everyone else. Mac was mercifully silent. Sarah didn't mind if he didn't say another word to her for the rest of the trip.

The brunette woman scanned Sarah's ticket and gave her a smile. "Have a pleasant flight."

Sarah smiled back.

Temporary.

This was a round-trip flight. Her job would be waiting for her, if she could get back in time. And if Mac got upset, she would remind him that she'd told him her plans right here at the airport. She would stay there while Mom got better. That was all she'd promised.

It wouldn't be hard to leave. It was only hard to go back.

CHAPTER THREE

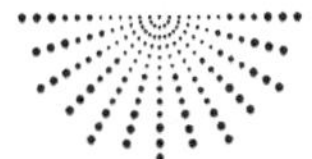

WILL

Will Brooks reminded himself that he was lucky. Lots of people would love to trade spots with him. He had the business. The wife. The money.

There was only one thing missing. It was a depressing realization that he'd avoided for a long time, but now that he was aware of it, there was no going back.

He didn't have what he truly wanted.

After ten years of marriage, Will was going to tell Rachel he was ready for kids. Year after year, they had pushed it off, and neither of them were getting any younger. If much more time passed, Will would barely be able to get up the stairs by the time the kids were old enough to walk.

Will ran a hand through his hair, something he did so often it was a miracle he wasn't bald already. He reached for his coffee. Empty.

With a sigh, he pushed himself up from the desk chair and made his way to the reception area. Bart trotted at his heels. The indeterminate terrier mix hadn't strayed from

Will's side since he'd found the dog poking around a dumpster in downtown Seattle several years ago.

Will peered around the corner to make sure the coast was clear. There was no sight of his office manager, Cindy.

He scurried across the room and sloshed coffee into his cup before hightailing it back to his office. Will liked Cindy. She kept this place running like a well-oiled machine. But if she saw him, she'd bug him about skipping meals again. He didn't want to lose his patience with Cindy when he knew Rachel was the one who'd planted the idea in her head.

Will cracked his neck and lowered himself back into his desk chair. Bart settled in beside him, resting his wiry head on Will's boot. Will reached down to scratch his ears, certain every dog was a therapy dog. How he'd made it through a day before Bart came into his life, Will couldn't remember.

He frowned as he reviewed a work order for another hire. He'd need Jason's input on this. Will was the voice of reason, concerned by numbers and projections while his business partner and best friend, Jason, was comfortable with risks. Together, they balanced each other out. If it hadn't been for Jason, Will doubted the business would've ever moved beyond the two of them. But if it hadn't been for Will, they probably would've gone bankrupt by now.

Except Jason was almost never around the office these days. He had to be dating someone new, because Will had learned that the less he saw of Jason, the more some woman certainly did. He felt guilty he hadn't sat down and checked in with his friend for a while.

The call rang. Once. Twice. Will had resigned himself to leave a voicemail when Jason finally picked up.

"Will? What's going on? Everything okay?" Jason's words came out rapid-fire.

Jason still worked in the field with the guys. He couldn't stand being behind a desk. It wasn't Will's favorite either, but someone had to do it. He only wished he could've kept his hard-earned muscles like Jason had. Will resembled his gangly teenage self more and more these days. "I'm fine. Just wanted to call you about a new hire. Can you give me an update about what's going on out there?"

"Oh," Jason breathed into the phone, his voice dropping an octave. "I thought this was about Rachel."

Will sighed. Jason was a better friend than he deserved. "No. We're not meeting until later. Trust me, I'll tell you how that goes."

"Right, right, you're having dinner tonight. It's your anniversary, isn't it?"

Will chuckled. "See? That's why I picked you for my best man."

Jason's laugh was awkward as he brought the conversation back to work.

When Will ended the call, his cell phone beeped with a reminder about his dinner reservations at one of the nicest restaurants in Seattle. Will hadn't forgotten. He pulled open his desk drawer, his eyes landing on a jewelry box that held a pair of diamond earrings.

Hopefully, Rachel liked them. Will wasn't sure what she liked these days, and that included him, but he would know where he stood tonight.

Will hadn't minded paying for their expensive life with years of his own while Rachel got her nails done and slept in. He'd thought he was providing for a family.

During the first few years of dating, they'd used to daydream about what they would name their kids. After they'd gotten married, Rachel had assured Will she wanted children, but that they'd needed time to get established. Then Will had been busy with the business, and Rachel had been busy rebuilding her body. By the time he had enough staff to provide him with free time, she was too concerned about undoing the work of several plastic surgeons.

But Will was ready for kids, with or without his wife. He was ready to be the bad guy. And the diamond earrings? Either a celebration of their marriage or a parting gift. That was up to Rachel. Today wasn't an anniversary.

It was a deadline.

* * *

WILL MADE it through the pile of permits, tossing the last one in the stack for Cindy to file. He leaned back in his chair and rubbed his eyes. He needed glasses.

Getting old sucked.

Will added the optometrist to his to-do list and checked the time. He had two hours until dinner. A suit was draped over a chair, ready for him to change into after work. He was going to meet Rachel at the restaurant. Will had asked her to meet him at the office so they could go together, but she'd said she had a hair appointment for their special night.

Rachel had a lot of appointments lately, though for what he couldn't imagine. She looked as beautiful as the day he'd married her.

A knock sounded at the door.

"What's up, Cindy?" he called out.

The door opened, and the scent of gardenias filled the room.

He frowned as Rachel stepped into his office. Her waist-length chestnut hair looked exactly the same as it had the last time he saw her.

Will stood. "I thought I was meeting you at the restaurant. Our reservation isn't for two more hours."

"I know." She pushed her sunglasses back, her ice-blue

eyes taking in his appearance. "Don't tell me you've spent all day here? I'll bet fifty dollars you haven't eaten either."

Will shrugged. He was tired of arguing with her. "But it would really be me betting against myself. It's all my money."

She let out a huff. "As you remind me every time."

His gaze flicked back to his desk. Maybe it was a good thing she'd stopped by. After all, he'd waited long enough for an answer. "I could probably take the rest of the day off, if you want to start the night early. We can get a drink somewhere and wait for the reservation."

She closed the door behind her. "I recommend you sit down."

Will didn't move.

Rachel reached into her designer bag and grabbed a manila envelope, handing it to him. "Fine. Have it your way. Don't know why I'm surprised."

Will worked the flap free. "What's this?"

"There's no easy way to say this. I want a divorce."

Will had played football in high school. He'd never been great, just average, but Rachel had encouraged him to go out for the team. In his junior year, they had substituted him in at the last minute. His school had been up against the best team in the district, and Will had taken a hit so hard he'd seen stars.

He was experiencing a similar feeling now.

"You want a what?" he stuttered.

She flicked her hair over her shoulder. "A divorce. This, us, we're not happy."

Any shred of guilt he'd felt about asking Rachel for kids shriveled up as his brain absorbed the information. So now he knew her answer. Wasn't that what he'd wanted? "Why?"

She raised a sculpted eyebrow. "Shouldn't you be asking what? Or who?"

As his blood pressure went up, his patience went down.

He couldn't imagine a worse time for her stupid games. "God dammit, what do you mean?"

"As in, what do I want or who am I leaving you for?"

Will snorted. "I guess that answers why."

She crossed her arms, manicured hands resting delicately on her elbows. "I'm going to need money. A lot. Thanks to the lifestyle you provided me, it should make my plea for alimony pretty easy."

Will blinked. Was she out of her damn mind? "Money?"

She smiled, full lips curling back to reveal white veneers. "Money. I know you have it."

Will choked back a laugh. She was definitely nuts. "You're on all my bank accounts. You know how much money there is."

Rachel picked an invisible piece of lint off her crisply ironed pants. "Don't screw with me, Will. I know there has to be more. There's no way you could have this business and not have it."

He ran his hand through his hair. Rachel had always had impossible expectations. "Open your eyes. It's tied up in the business, the condo, the cars, our retirement accounts. I don't keep everything in a coffee can out back. There's not a pile of cash I can transfer to you."

Rachel cocked her head to the side. "He said you might say something like that."

Will clenched his jaw. "Who's he?"

She ignored his question. "So I am going to need something else then. I'm going to need your shares in the business."

The laugh escaped. "You're bat shit crazy."

"I'm doing you a favor," she cooed. "You won't want to come to work every day after the dust settles."

Will narrowed his eyes. "Why the hell wouldn't I want to come to the business I've built every day?"

"Don't you get it?" She scoffed. "I can't believe you haven't put the pieces together yet. It's Jason."

The stars swimming in his vision made a painful return.

It couldn't be. His best friend. His best man. His business partner? When Rachel screwed someone, she didn't play around. He would gladly take a football helmet to the stomach if it could erase Rachel's words.

Then pieces started falling into place. Rachel's boredom with Will. All her appointments. The fact that Will hadn't seen Jason around in forever.

He'd suspected his friend had a new woman, he just hadn't thought it'd be his own wife.

"Jason," he repeated, the name sounding strange to his own ears. "So you're telling me while I sat here day in and day out, you two were getting cozy?"

She smiled. "You're not as stupid as you look."

His shoulders sagged. "We could've had kids by now."

She shuddered. "Thank goodness we don't. That would only make this more messy."

Will's disbelief morphed into rage as the fog lifted. All these years had meant nothing to her? This would be the last time he trusted a pretty face.

Bart whimpered behind him, and Rachel's eyes locked on the small dog.

"I want him too. I've spent more time with him than you. I took care of him when he got that infection, remember?"

Will gritted his teeth. "Why the hell would you want my dog? You don't even want kids."

She stuck her chin out. "Our dog. You got him while we were together."

He picked up Bart, wrapping his arms around him. Like hell she was taking his dog. "You can go screw yourself, Rachel."

"You can't talk to me like that!" She screamed in his face, her cool demeanor gone.

Bile rose in the back of his throat. This was the woman he'd married? "I honestly can't talk to you at all right now. Get out. I'll see you in court."

She stomped away, slamming the door shut behind her.

The office closed in around him. Each year, each day he had wasted on Rachel weighing down on him, threatening to flatten him to the floor.

He shoved his truck keys into his pocket. Still holding Bart with one arm, Will ripped the drawer open and grabbed the diamond earrings with the other.

He stepped into the reception area to see Cindy doing her best impression of being busy.

"Merry Christmas." Will slammed the jewelry box on her desk. "Please cancel my dinner reservations. I'm leaving for the rest of the day."

She looked up at him with wide eyes.

"And find me a lawyer!" He yelled over his shoulder.

That bitch was not taking his dog.

CHAPTER FOUR

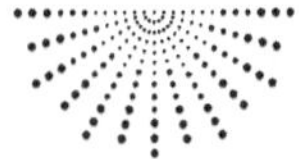

WILL

Will paced outside the attorney's office, the gray, drizzly weather a perfect reflection of his mood. He stomped in the puddles as he walked up and down the street, his anger growing. He just wanted to get this over with.

He had thought about it long and hard after talking to Rachel that day. He knew she would go after him for all he was worth, but Will would fight back just as hard. They had always been equally stubborn. Compromise in their relationship had consisted of Will giving in to keep Rachel happy. But not this time.

With a sinking sense of dread, he could see the writing on the wall. Rachel had never made a dime for herself. It had started with Will paying for their dates in high school with money he'd earned with his job at the hardware store. That had led to him helping her with tuition, covering the rent for their first apartment and putting the down payment on the condo with money from his bank account. Every dinner, pair of shoes, and car payment had been paid for with a credit card with his name on it. He had a feeling she wouldn't be walking away with nothing in the separation. Rachel always got her way.

In the end, they had decided on mediation. Will didn't want this to drag out for months. Every time he thought about the situation, he felt sick. He hadn't been happy in the marriage for a while now, and clearly Rachel had felt the same way. Will was ready to move on. After all, Rachel had gotten what she wanted in the end. Why shouldn't he?

A car door slammed, and Will snapped his head up.

Rachel stepped out of the luxury sedan in a bright pink rain coat, with a matching umbrella held over her head.

He looked down at his own black slicker. Rachel looked ready for a party, and Will looked ready for a funeral.

Someone came around from the other side of the car to stand beside her.

Will's jaw dropped as he watched the two of them walk up hand-in-hand. There was no way. "What the hell is he doing here?"

"Don't be rude, William. You know we're together now." Rachel chided him.

"Hey Will." Jason flicked his gaze up just for a moment before casting it back down on the sidewalk. At least he had the decency to act embarrassed.

"Shall we?" Rachel asked, as if they were about to be seated for brunch rather than neatly snip their lives apart.

They crowded into the reception area where the attorney mercifully told Jason that he needed to wait outside. Will hoped that wouldn't be his only victory of the day.

Rachel moaned and groaned, and Will resisted the urge to remind her she and Will were the ones married, not her and Jason. He figured that wouldn't help negotiations.

Besides, it was fair. He couldn't have Bart with him, and he hadn't let the dog out of his sight since Rachel had added him to her divorce wishlist. Will hoped he wasn't giving Cindy too much trouble at the office, but he hadn't wanted to take him to a kennel. Will knew he was in no shape to resist Bart's pleading eyes if he'd tried to drop him off at dog daycare.

As requested, Will and Rachel had provided a list of all their assets and mutual property.

They would each keep their vehicles. Will's truck had been paid off for years now, and he had just bought out the lease for Rachel's sedan.

"The condo?" The attorney asked.

Rachel gave a wave of her hand. "I'm going to need Will to buy me out. I'm moving in with Jason."

Will flinched. Just like that, she grabbed the knife and twisted it. "You're moving in together?"

"I basically live there already," she said in a clipped tone.

Will's body grew hot. He turned back to the attorney. "For the record, she cheated on me. Why should I have to give her anything?"

The attorney held up his hands. "Washington is a no-fault state."

Will cursed under his breath. "Jesus Christ. Sell the damn condo. I don't care. Pain in the ass to take the dog outside, anyway."

The attorney cleared his throat. "Now to alimony. Though Mrs. Brooks has presented a buy out option…"

"Let me stop you right there," Will interrupted. "There is no money. It's all tied up in the business. The only thing left is our retirement accounts, you know that. It's all on that list. I had Cindy send over the financial statements from the company, too."

The attorney shuffled the papers, tapping them into a tidy stack. "The buy out option isn't for cash. She wants shares in the company."

"I told you," she said in a singsong voice next to him.

Will's blood boiled. "How much? How many shares?"

"She wants your half."

"My half?" He choked on the question.

The attorney adjusted his glasses. "Yes. The company is equally divided between you and Jason Maxwell. She wants your ownership, thus making her and Mr. Maxwell one-hundred percent owners."

Will covered his face with his hands. What a damned nightmare. The only thing keeping him from completely losing it was that he had another option. "I'm sorry, I am just trying to understand. And what's the alimony amount?"

The attorney named a number so staggering that it made the high-rise condo look like a bargain, even in the astronomical Seattle real estate market. "I promise if you take this to court, it will be at least that much. If not more. Plus, your time and money spent on legal proceedings."

Will's mouth went dry. So much for options. "Can I have time to think about it?"

"Jason and I have waited long enough to be together." Rachel crossed her arms. "If you make me wait any longer, I'm taking you to court."

He leaned towards her, the smell of the perfume he'd bought her in Paris turning his stomach. "Look sweetheart, I can't just sign everything over to you today. It's a multi-million dollar business, not a newspaper route. I have other loopholes I have to go through."

"I'm willing to wait a week." She sniffed, then placed a hand on his knee. "Don't worry. You can still be an employee."

Will stood so abruptly that the chair wobbled. He couldn't be in this room for one more second. He turned to the attorney. "I'm done here. I'll call you with my decision in the morning."

He brushed past Rachel and made his way out the front door without saying a word to Jason.

"William, wait!" His soon-to-be ex-wife called after him, her heels smacking on the wet sidewalk. "I have something for you."

He spun around to face her, his jaw clenched. "You're giving me something? Now this I gotta see. Here I thought all you knew how to do was take."

"No need to be an ass about it," she muttered. Rachel reached into her purse and pulled out something that looked like a postcard. "Here."

Will accepted the paper, a thick textured cardstock, the kind that felt expensive. His stomach sank to his knees. He saw Rachel and Jason's names, a photo of the two of them smiling.

His mind struggled to make sense of the whole thing. This wasn't happening. "Save the date?"

She smiled. "You know, for a wedding. We did them for ours, remember?"

Will gaped at her. "Are you seriously using our wedding as a point of reference for whatever this is?"

Rachel narrowed her eyes. "Jason and I are getting married. We're in love. I already told you back in the attorney's office. We've waited long enough."

His head spun. Will didn't know what to say. He shoved the invitation into his back pocket and walked away.

Rachel yelled something after him, but Will couldn't understand her. His ears roared, the sound of a man sinking deeper and deeper.

He was almost to his truck when the sound of rapid footsteps and splashing water drew his attention.

Jason jogged up, completely at ease, his breathing steady. Will would gasp like a fish out of water if he had to jog a block. His anger grew at the realization of just how much he had sacrificed only to be betrayed by the people he cared about most. "Will, wait. Please. Can I talk to you?"

Will opened the truck door. He had nothing to say to his former best friend. "I think it's best if any communication between me and the two of you is done through the attorney."

Jason hung his head. "I'm sorry. I didn't mean for it to happen this way. I've known Rachel as long as you have. We've spent a lot of time together. It's not like I just met her and stole her out from under your nose."

Will cracked his neck. "Oh really? Explain to me how you meant for it to happen?"

"Look, man. She was lonely. You were always at work. You never wanted to do anything. I did. Maybe Rachel and I are just a better match, that's all. Doesn't mean we can't still be friends. We've been through a lot over the years. We can get through this, too."

Will couldn't believe what he was hearing. "You don't get it, do you? I was busy being boring behind a desk, so Rachel got bored. It's going to happen again, and you'll find yourself right back in this office. Except this time, you'll get to join in on the appointment."

With that, Will turned the key and drove away the second the ignition roared to life. He pushed the V8 to its limit as he peeled down the street, speed limit be damned. At that moment, nothing mattered more than getting far, far away.

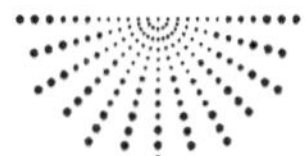

WILL

Will went straight to the office to pick up Bart from Cindy. She opened her mouth, took one look at Will's face, and said nothing. Fine by him. He didn't want to talk to a single person today, and definitely not to a woman. In fact, he didn't care if he never spoke to another female again. Nothing good ever came of it.

On his way home, Will bought a six-pack and a bottle of his favorite Scotch, intending to make it all disappear by sunup tomorrow. What else did he have to do, anyway? Rachel had taken his life apart brick by brick, leaving him with nothing but rubble.

After a quick potty break for Bart, they took the elevator to their floor. Inside the condo, Will filled the dog's food bowl before helping himself to his first beer. He tossed the bottle cap on the countertop, something Rachel used to always nag him about. But who cared anymore? Rachel wasn't here.

Will walked through the condo in a daze. Empty hangers in her closet. Most of her makeup, gone. Not a single pair of shoes left. How could he not have noticed?

He gulped his beer. He had been working non-stop to fund Rachel and Jason's dream wedding. That's how he hadn't noticed.

Will massaged the back of his neck. Maybe he had done this. Was Rachel lonely like Jason had said? Was that what had happened?

Pulling out his phone, he scrolled through his calendar. There were at least five canceled date nights, and Will hadn't been the one to cancel them. Maybe he could've done more, but then again, she could have, too. It took two to tango.

He tossed the empty bottle in recycling and grabbed another, hoping the second beer would improve his mood. Right now, he felt somewhere between furious and ready to vomit.

Will wandered to the window. The weather outside looked worse than earlier. Shit, he probably had seasonal affective disorder on top of everything else. These stupid floor-to-ceiling windows meant he never got away from the constant rain and gray sky. They paid a pretty penny for the view from the top floor, and there were very few days in a year when Will truly got to enjoy it. The whole thing was indicative of his life.

He ran his hand down his face. Will wanted none of this. He didn't like this condo. It was a pain to take Bart outside. He couldn't have a barbecue. And, to be honest, it had never felt like home. It was sleek, and modern, and uncomfortable. None of this was Will's style. He hadn't wanted fancy cars. or five course meals, or all-inclusive vacations.

What he wanted was a family.

Bart nuzzled up against his ankle, warming Will's heart.

At least he wasn't completely alone. Will kneeled down to scratch the dog's floppy ears.

His phone beeped with a reminder of a work meeting tomorrow. He tossed the phone on the couch. Maybe he didn't even need to go. It might be Rachel and Jason's problem soon.

His head throbbed. If he gave Rachel what she wanted, then what would he do for work? He had been running the business for years, and he hadn't done physical labor for a long, long time. But he had to make a living somehow, and construction was all he knew.

And forget about relationships. He was never dating again.

Will reached into his back pocket and pulled out the save the date Rachel had given him. He should want to tear it up. Hold a lighter under it. Shove it in the garbage disposal. But somehow, looking at the picture of the two people he had trusted the most in the world made it very easy to think clearly.

Heading back to the kitchen, Will grabbed another beer and cracked open the whisky. He settled onto the couch, where Bart hopped up to snuggle next to him.

Will weighed his options. He could pay alimony. But that meant a continuous connection to Rachel, plus pressure for the business to remain successful. Just thinking about it gave him a stress headache.

Or he could give her what she wanted. Let Rachel and Jason run the business. She said they were in love, but being in business together was different. Rachel must've forgotten all the fights Will and Jason had had about the company over the years.

That was assuming either of them knew how to do what he did. Will would bet money they couldn't even file a permit without Cindy's help.

He went back into the kitchen for his third beer. Or was it his fourth? Either way, a six-pack had been far from enough.

Will massaged his forehead, wishing there was someone he could call to get good and drunk with to figure this all out. That person had always been Jason.

Will let out a short laugh. Rachel had really taken everything from him. He was royally screwed.

He wandered into the kitchen and brought the bottle of whisky back to the couch with him.

Will was over the games, and the pretending, and the fights. He was ready to put this behind him. He didn't want to pay alimony to Rachel until his dying day, and he sure as heck would not work for her.

He tipped his head back, emptying his glass. The whisky whispered an idea to him, and Will listened.

* * *

WILL LET OUT A MOAN, blinking one eye open and then the other. The sun had made a rare appearance, and the living room was flooded with light. Almost as rare as Will sleeping in. His cheek made a sucking sound as he peeled himself off the leather couch.

Head pounding, he took in the empty beer bottles and almost empty bottle of whisky that littered the floor. His laptop sat open on the coffee table.

What was that doing out?

He tapped on the keys, but the battery was dead.

Bart sat in front of him, whining. Will checked the time, his eyes almost popping out of his head. "I'm so sorry, boy. Let's go."

Will didn't even bother with the leash. The HOA might

fine him, but Will didn't care. Bart never left his side, anyway.

After Bart had had his break, Will came back inside and took a scalding shower. Next, he cleaned up the empty bottles, his stomach turning at the smell of stale beer.

With a shudder, he realized he'd hit a low point. At least it couldn't get worse.

Will shot Cindy a text that he would be in later. He had a stop to make first.

Grabbing a black coffee and a bagel, Will headed to the attorney's office. The attorney was in court, so Will left a message with his assistant. Now that he had decided what to do, he wanted it done as soon as possible.

He stopped at a hardware store and bought some boxes and packaging tape before getting to the office.

Cindy eyed him warily when he walked in. "Are you okay?"

Will rubbed his temples. "No, not at all. I'm hungover. Rachel and Jason are getting married. And, oh yeah, she's also getting my half of the company."

Cindy's jaw dropped. "Oh God, I'm so sorry. I don't know what to say."

"Nothing for you to be sorry about. I'm just sorry you're going to be working for an ice queen. You might want to find a new job. I'm not sure either of them can file a permit on their own."

"Sounds like they're going to have to learn," she said in a crisp tone.

"Why don't you put together a severance package for yourself? I can get it signed before all this goes through."

She gave him a sympathetic smile. "You're a good guy. I hope you know that."

He sighed. "Not good enough, apparently."

Despite his churning stomach, Will made quick work of

packing up his office. There wasn't as much personal stuff as he'd thought, and he even had a few extra boxes. He would save those for Cindy. He'd known she was a smart one. Her jumping ship proved it.

As he cleared out his desk drawers, his cell phone rang.

"This is Sarah Carter from the Salmonberry Lodge. I'm trying to reach William Brooks."

Will frowned. He'd never heard of the place. "This is he. How can I help you?"

"You sent in an application about the handyman job?"

He lowered himself down into his desk chair, his headache worsening. "The what?"

The woman on the phone talked faster, her words jumbled together. "I know you just applied, but we really need someone as soon as possible. I was hoping to set up an interview. By phone, of course."

Will suddenly had a suspicion about what his laptop had been doing out this morning. Not that he remembered much from last night. "Sure, okay. When's a good time?"

"Are you free tomorrow?"

"Just a minute, let me check my schedule."

Will put Sarah on speaker phone and pulled up a search for Salmonberry Lodge on his phone.

He blinked. That couldn't be right. There was only one result, a webpage that looked like it had been last updated in 1995. "Is this the Salmonberry Lodge in Alaska?"

"It's the only one I know about," the woman said.

"I'll take it."

"You'll take the job?" She asked. "But you haven't even interviewed."

"I thought you wanted someone to start immediately?"

"It's hard to pass up on someone with so much experience," she murmured. "Do you have any questions for me?"

There was only one question that mattered. "Are there any women there?"

She hesitated. "Very few and most are over fifty."

"Then sign me up. Unless you have anyone else to interview."

A second passed, and then another.

The woman sighed. "Welcome to the Salmonberry Lodge."

CHAPTER SIX

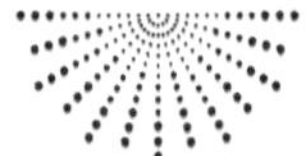

SARAH

Sarah tugged her ponytail loose and made another attempt at putting her hair up. The shoulder-length cut that had seemed stylish in California was a nuisance here. While she worked around the lodge, her hair flopped in front of her eyes and tickled her nose. She wasn't spending all day sitting at a desk anymore. This place had done more for her fitness routine than all her best attempts in LA.

Sarah stretched her arms overhead and let out a moan. Her shoulders ached from the hours spent scrubbing every inch of the lodge. There wasn't a speck of dust in the whole place.

She couldn't wait for her parents to see it. The lodge was her parent's pride and joy, second only to their children. Over the years, they'd turned it into a beautiful property, and they'd prided themselves on keeping it pristine. When Sarah had left it had looked ready for a calendar picture. But that had been five years ago.

She'd been speechless the first time she saw it after returning from California.

Even if Mac hadn't told Sarah about her mom's accident, she would have known something was wrong. The place had been a mess. Not just a mess. It had practically been falling apart.

Mac had given her a sideways glance. "Told you."

Sarah had swallowed, but the lump in her throat had refused to move. "Are there any guests?"

"No. Not good timing, either. We need this right now."

Sarah had hoped coming back here would assuage her guilt, but in a frustrating twist of fate, it had only made it worse.

She massaged her temples. What mattered now was getting the lodge up and running again, and stewing on the past wouldn't help that. Sarah glanced around the room as she mentally recited her to-do list. What should she tackle next?

Her stomach growled, deciding for her. She had been surviving on black coffee and an apple all day. She grabbed one of her mom's cookbooks and thumbed through the pages until she found the one she was looking for.

She bit her lip as she skimmed the recipe. Her mom had written in the margins, adjusting the amounts for a triple batch. The lodge was all-inclusive, which meant three home-made meals a day.

Sarah let out a sigh. She hadn't turned on the oven in her condo once. Cooking from scratch for the entire summer? That would take a miracle.

Setting aside the cookbook, Sarah pulled out her cell phone and tapped on her dad's name.

"Hi, sweetheart. Everything going okay?" he whispered. Her mom must be sleeping, just like the last time Sarah had gone over there.

"I'm making dinner and wondered if you wanted me to bring you some? There will be a ton of leftovers. That way you and Mom don't have to cook tonight."

"That's really thoughtful, honey, but your mom is sleeping right now. I'm not sure when she's going to get up. These pain meds have her all over the place. Maybe next time?"

"Yeah, of course."

Sarah slipped the phone back into her pocket, frowning. After years of asking her to come back, her parents acted like she was still in California. Sarah had only seen them once so far.

She felt a twinge of guilt. Her mom was hurt. Who cared if she slept all day? That was probably for the best.

Sarah shook the guilt off and focused on making dinner. She tossed together an olive oil and lemon marinade, then added chicken to the large bowl. While that sat in the fridge, she prepped greens and cubed sweet potatoes. It only took three instructional videos online to get her through those first few steps.

She arranged everything on a sheet pan before sliding it into the oven. Sarah set a timer and then grabbed a loaf of homemade sourdough from the freezer to make garlic bread. It was a bit untraditional, but hopefully the handyman wasn't too picky.

A door slammed followed by boots thumping on the porch. Her shoulders pinched together. Sarah didn't have to check the grandfather clock in the entryway to know her big brother was right on time. Mac always did what he said he'd do. It was beyond annoying.

He walked in the front door and looked around. "Looks good."

Sarah bit her tongue. Trust her brother to sum up a week of hard work in two words.

"So you've got a pickup in Ketchikan on the books today?

We don't need to chat before every one of these. I know you're out of practice, so I just want to remind you." He gave her a grin that said she could eat shit.

Sarah didn't take the bait. Mac hadn't forgiven her for leaving in the first place, and he never would. She refused to indulge him. "Duly noted. We don't need to talk every time you have a pickup for the lodge. Here's the thing. You're not picking up a guest."

Mac's eyebrows squished together. "What?"

Sarah clasped her hands in front of her, rocking on her feet. She knew this would go over like a lead balloon. "Well, he's sort of a guest. But he's also not?"

Mac tugged on his beard. "Jesus, save that wishy-washy shit for California. Say what you mean and mean what you say."

"I hired someone to help with the lodge this summer," she spat out.

"You what?" Mac's voice was quiet.

Sarah swallowed. She hated when Mac used his quiet voice. "I hired someone. Don't worry, you cheapskate. I'm paying him myself."

Mac cracked his knuckles. "Are you serious?"

Sarah threw her arms in the air. "What's so bad about that?"

"Jesus Sarah, this is a family business!" Even though he yelled loud enough for the entire island to hear him, Sarah saw it as progress. At least he wasn't totally pissed.

She put her hands on her hips. Mac may have dragged her back from California, but he was delusional if he thought he could push her around all summer. "Yeah, and the family needs help. Mom and Dad can't do anything this summer. You know as well as I do what this place looked like when I arrived. You told me yourself that you don't have the time to do anything but flights."

He shook his head. "There has to be another way."

Sarah stretched her arms wide, gesturing to the lodge. "There isn't. Look around, Mac. The porch is sagging. The faucets are leaking. You can get splinters from the handrail. Come on. We need this, remember?"

Mac's green gaze held her own. "This better not be another classic Sarah mistake."

She hurried after him as he stomped out the front door, practically tripping over her own feet. He couldn't just say something like that and walk away. "What the hell does that mean?"

Mac stepped one foot inside the cab. "It means we all have to pay for it."

The truck roared out of the driveway, leaving Sarah with only Mac's words and the smell of diesel.

Her stomach twisted. She didn't know what it had been like for them after she left. She tried not to think about it.

But Mac didn't know what it was like for her, either.

Her brother thought living in California was a fate worse than death. He didn't know that Darling was the place she had nightmares about. So in the end, he'd come up with the perfect punishment for her, after all.

When she'd left, everyone had assumed she had been grieving for her lost love. In a way, she had been. But no one knew the full truth. No one knew that she, Sarah Lynn Carter, had killed Andre. And nothing would ever bring him back.

CHAPTER SEVEN

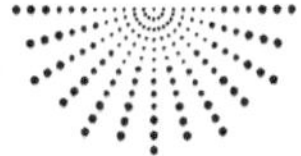

WILL

Will shifted from foot to foot as he waited at the Ketchikan airport, where his flight from Seattle had arrived half an hour ahead of schedule. The woman from the lodge had told him that someone would pick him up here. When Will had asked for details, she had laughed. "You can't miss him. He definitely won't miss you."

Will was jealous of her easygoing attitude. He wondered what it was like when not everything in life felt hard.

He stuck his hand in his back pocket and felt the card stock folded in half. It had been a last-minute decision to grab the wedding invitation when he'd left. He'd thought it might come in handy if he ever needed to remind himself why he'd come to Alaska.

He had set everything up with the attorney's office before he'd boarded the plane, but he'd left a forwarding address just in case there was anything that still needed his signature. If Will had it his way, he wouldn't go back to Seattle until the divorce was final. Or maybe he would never go back. There wasn't much to go back to.

He looked around the airport, taking in the tall rain boots and plastic jackets. He stood out like a sore thumb in jeans that still held their color and hiking boots that had never actually been on a mountain trail. It was one of the million activities he'd had great intentions to do but had never found the time for. Maybe he would try it out now that he had the opposite problem. Plenty of time with nothing to do.

Will scanned the area again for his ride. He checked his watch, noting twenty minutes had passed. He hoped this whole thing wasn't a scam. Apparently, he was easy to fool.

With a sigh, he grabbed his duffel bag and was about to go get a cup of coffee from the airport cafe when a man appeared, making a beeline towards him. The man was easily the tallest person in the room, wide as a door, and with a face that said he wasn't there to make friends.

The giant stopped short in front of him. "You William Brooks?"

Will gave a firm nod.

The man pointed to the ground. "That your bag?"

Without waiting for an answer, the giant grabbed the duffel bag and flung it over his shoulder like it weighed no more than a fanny pack. He walked away, leaving Will to scramble after him.

Will tried to keep the dog carrier steady as he ran to catch up. "Excuse me…"

With a sigh, the man stopped and faced Will. "You're going to the Salmonberry Lodge, right?"

"That's right."

"Well then, I'm your ride." The man bared his teeth. Was he trying to smile? Bart whined, and the man eyed the carrier. "You brought a dog?"

It didn't sound like a question to Will. "Sarah said it would be fine."

The man rolled his eyes. "Whatever. That's her problem."

"You'll barely notice him." Will held up the carrier. "He's pretty small."

The man peered at Bart. "Looks like an eagle snack to me."

He turned again, leaving Will staring behind him. Will glanced at the sky, an empty gray expanse. Bart whined, and Will stuck a finger into the carrier to reassure him with a scratch. Surely the giant was joking. But then again, Bart barely weighed five pounds, and eagles could carry a whole salmon. Couldn't they?

Will squared his shoulders. He had protected Bart from his wife's talons. Surely an eagle couldn't present that much more of a challenge.

* * *

WILL CRAWLED INSIDE THE FLOATPLANE, hoping this guy knew what he was doing.

The man gave Will a quick safety rundown before takeoff. "Any questions?"

"What's your name?" Will asked.

"Mac," the man spat out. He kept his gaze trained forward, not bothering to spare Will a sideways glance.

Will let out a sigh, resting his head on the seat back. Maybe customer service was different in Alaska, too. Or maybe coming here in the first place had been a mistake.

The plane started up, and Mac guided them across the water. Will watched his every movement while keeping a firm hold on Bart's carrier in his lap. A constant rain splattered against the windshield instead of snow, the humid air thick.

Once they were in the air, Will all but pressed his nose to the window. Endless islands dotted the dark waters, covered with thick trees that ended only where the rocky beaches began. There was nothing but nature, a land humanity had politely overlooked in the civilization of the world.

They began their descent, heading towards one of the larger islands Will had seen. He could pick out a few buildings, but saw nothing that would qualify as a lodge or a town. This wasn't in the middle of nowhere. It *was* nowhere.

Will swallowed. Suddenly Seattle seemed very far away.

Mac landed the plane with the skill of a man who had done it a thousand times before.

Will felt dizzy with relief. They had made it.

Mac hopped out of the plane without a word. Will followed his lead, clutching Bart to his chest as he took a cautious step onto the bobbing dock.

The pilot threw the duffel bag over his shoulder, heading in the direction of a truck that looked older than God. "Come on, city slicker. We're not there yet."

After twenty minutes of bumping along an unpaved road, Mac took a turn, and the sign for the Salmonberry Lodge came into view.

After Mac pulled to a stop in front of the lodge, Will tried to get out, but the rusted door didn't budge. In a fit of frustration, he shoved the door with his foot. It was reluctant to let him out, moaning as it moved. Will carefully set Bart on the ground and grabbed his bag from the back of the truck before sweeping his dog back into his arms.

Mac didn't even bother to unbuckle his seatbelt, let alone offer to help. "Let me know when you need a ride back."

He pulled out of the driveway, the gravel crunching beneath the tires.

Will's stomach jumped around as he watched the truck grow smaller. He had no idea what he was in for. Not even a month ago, he'd had a business, a marriage, what he thought was a life. Now it was just him, his dog, and a suitcase on an island in Alaska where the locals made bears seem friendly. Hopefully this wasn't a huge mistake. He didn't seem to be on a winning streak lately.

Will took a deep breath and reached into his back pocket, his fingers clamping on the thick cardstock of the wedding invitation. There was no going back.

* * *

THE FRONT STEPS creaked under his weight, and Will winced. When he knocked on the door, there was no answer. He knocked again, harder this time. He waited a few more minutes before deciding it was easier to ask forgiveness and eased the door open.

A billow of smoke rolled into his face, and his nose burned. He couldn't see a damn thing. An icy trail of dread crawled down his back.

The lodge was on fire.

"Is anyone in there?" he called out.

"Oh God!" a woman yelled. "Shit!"

He broke out in a sweat. Someone was in there, and as far as Will knew, he was the only other person around.

Will's hands shook as he set Bart down on the edge of the porch. Will wasn't sure what wild creatures might be interested in his dog, but he didn't think bringing him into a burning house was a better alternative.

With a cough, Will pulled his t-shirt up over his nose and stepped through the front door. His eyes burned and watered as he choked on the smoke.

Bright yellow flames licked out from across the room. Fighting his instincts, he moved closer to the fire, letting out a curse as he bumped into a heavy dining table.

He spotted a woman, frozen in place.

Will cupped his hands together. "Hello!"

No response.

His heart beat once. Twice. The flames reached for the woman again.

Will moved faster than the fire, wrapped his arms around the woman's waist, and pulled her to the side. Grabbing a towel, he doused it in water, and threw it over the source of the fire.

The flaming sheet pan sputtered as it transformed from a blaze to stinky black smoke.

Wiping at his eyes, Will turned to the woman. "Are you okay?"

She stood so still Will wondered if she was in shock. He took a step towards her, and reached out a hand.

"I'm fine." She wrapped her arms around herself. "But your dinner isn't. So much for a special first day."

"Sarah?" Will asked.

She nodded, and for the first time since running inside, Will noticed more than simply the fact that she was a woman. Her pale face was covered in a sheen of sweat and grime, making her green eyes stand out. The stains dotting her sweatshirt couldn't detract from the auburn hair escaping from her ponytail.

Will's mouth went dry. Sarah was drop dead gorgeous. Sweaty, dirty, and still beautiful. He couldn't imagine what she looked like on a good day.

He cleared his throat. "It's okay. I had a big meal on the plane."

Sarah laughed, and he was instantly addicted to the sound. "You're a horrible liar. I've taken that flight more than once in my lifetime, and I know they don't serve food. I doubt you had anything on the way here. This isn't exactly the capital of gourmet dining."

"Fine, you win," Will smiled. "But at least the man who picked me up was efficient."

"That's being polite. But that's Mac for you. Take him or leave him. He doesn't care either way."

"So you know him?" Will asked, praying the two of them had nothing to do with each other. It was obvious Mac didn't like him.

Sarah smoothed back a few escaped strands of hair, but they immediately popped free again. Will found it oddly endearing. "Unfortunately. He's my brother."

Will sighed. It was just his luck. "I don't think he's my biggest fan."

She lifted one corner of her mouth. "The good news is that he only comes here to transfer guests. If you see him, it'll be quick. I'm the one you'll be sick of by the end of summer."

Will gulped. He doubted anyone could get sick of her heart-shaped face and full mouth. So much for swearing off women.

A chill came over him. Rachel had been gorgeous, too, and that hadn't meant a damn thing in the end. After all, Will knew what he wanted this time around. A summer fling with a beautiful woman in Alaska might be fun, but it wouldn't get him any closer to his goal of having a family.

This time, Will would do better. This time, he wouldn't be fooled.

CHAPTER EIGHT

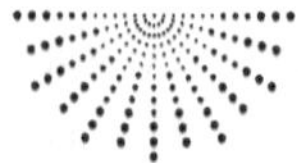

SARAH

Sarah rubbed her sides. The imprint of Will's arms wrapped around her burned into her skin. If she was going to almost set the lodge on fire, at least the timing had been lucky with a handyman there to save her.

Unluckily, he happened to be the sexiest man she'd seen in a long time. A long, long time. But his looks didn't matter. Sarah wasn't looking for romance. Not after what had happened the last time.

Will smiled, his blue eyes crinkling. "I'm glad you're okay."

Despite her best intentions, her heart skipped a beat. This was going to be interesting. "Thanks to you."

"I didn't realize this job included firefighting." He winked.

Sarah's shoulders bounced as a giggle escaped. "If you volunteer for that, people will never let you leave. The local brigade is ready to be retired." She clapped her hands together. "In the meantime, how about a tour? I'd offer you dinner, but…"

She looked at the smoking sheet pan. Seriously, could she do nothing right? Not that it mattered. Will would've figured out soon enough that she wasn't much of a cook. It was hard to keep secrets from someone you lived with.

A bark came from the front door, and Sarah raised an eyebrow.

"Sorry." Will headed towards the sound. "It's been a long day. He's normally pretty quiet."

Sarah followed Will. "If I had spent all day in a box and had to interact with Mac, I would bark too."

Back inside, Will opened the carrier, and a small wiry dog stepped out. "Sarah, meet Bart."

She knelt down to greet the dog. "Hey little guy."

Bart sniffed her palm, followed by a lick that made Sarah giggle. Then he wandered over to sniff one of the rustic log cabin arm chairs that sat in the entryway.

"Uh oh, he's showing a little too much interest. I think I better take him out for a minute." Will opened the front door and coaxed Bart outside. Sarah watched from the doorway as the scruffy white dog smelled around before lifting his leg.

Will walked briskly down the porch steps as he followed after Bart. He kept looking between the dog and the gray sky overhead.

"Everything okay?" Sarah asked.

Will knit his brows together. "Mac said something about Bart being an eagle snack. Part of me thinks he was joking, but another part of me isn't so sure."

She shook her head. Just because Mac wasn't happy Sarah had hired someone to help didn't give him the right to take it out on Will. "He was joking. Don't listen to him. If it were up to Mac, everyone would live unhappily ever after."

Bart ran back up to Will and sat by his feet.

Will looked up at Sarah and smiled. "So you said something about a tour? At the very least, can you show me which room is mine?"

Sarah felt her cheeks warm. It was tempting to give him a tour of her bed. She shoved the juvenile thought out of her mind. This was business, not pleasure.

They walked through the lower level of the lodge first, where Sarah showed him the kitchen, sitting room, and office. Then they went upstairs to the guest rooms and bathrooms.

"So not every room has its own bathroom," Will said. "That's European."

Sarah had forgotten that that wasn't the norm. Then again, neither was growing up at a lodge in Alaska. "I wouldn't know, never been. But so far, no complaints from the guests."

Will leaned against the doorway. "Sounds good to me. I'm okay with trying something new."

Sarah swallowed and looked away.

Will wasn't a fitness model, or an aspiring actor, or one of the million other stereotypes she had met on the daily in Los Angeles. He was older than her by at least a few years, and a few strands of gray mixed in with the dark brown hair at his temples. His clothes were too big, practically hanging off him. There was no reason she should feel anything towards him except thankful that he had taken the job. It had been pure luck to find someone with his years of experience at the last minute.

She tugged on the hem of her shirt. "I'm sure you're tired. I can show you to your room so you can rest up. It's getting late, and it might be awhile before dinner is ready."

Will shook his head. "I'm not tired. But let's start with the room."

Sarah pointed towards the end of the hallway. "Either of those have their own bathroom."

"I take it you charge more for those rooms?"

Sarah nodded. "We do. But I can't expect you to go all summer sharing a bathroom with random people."

"Is that what you're doing?"

She shrugged. "I'm used to it."

Will peeked into one of the smaller rooms. "What about this one?"

"Great view. Small space. No bathroom."

Will tilted his head. "Any chance I would share with Mac?"

Sarah laughed. "You'd be sharing with me."

"I can work with that if you can. I promise I take fast showers."

Heat crawled up her neck. The idea of him in the shower was distracting. "Then it sounds like we have a deal. You get settled in. I'm going to go downstairs to try to figure out dinner. Again."

He smiled. "I can't imagine a better first night in Alaska."

But her own stomach knotted as she made her way to the kitchen. Just another one of life's cruel jokes. It may be Will's first trip to Alaska, but for Sarah, it would be her last.

* * *

SARAH LET OUT a sigh as she opened the fridge door again. Like the last two times, there wasn't anything new to cook. It had turned out to be a good thing that her parents hadn't taken her up on her offer to bring them dinner. Sarah had frozen almost all the perishable groceries in the giant chest freezer that sat in the storeroom, and aside from scrambled eggs, she was out of ideas.

She eyed the bottles tucked snugly into the wine rack. Now that sounded like a good idea.

Sarah had expected to experience a lot of emotions when

she'd come back. She had been happy to see her parents again, and there was a cozy familiarity about being back on the island.

But she still felt the grief from Andre's death, guilt over having caused it, and anger that he had lied to her.

She felt it all so intensely it was as if the five years had never passed. As if it had all happened only yesterday.

Then there was the stress of not knowing whether or not she still had a job. Without her career, she had little to return to in California.

But there was a new emotion, too. One she hadn't expected.

Desire.

Sarah had been with her fair share of handsome men, but they had been just that. It had been no more than a physical attraction—they'd been a distraction more than anything else. She knew in her heart that she would never feel about anyone the way she had about Andre. And she preferred it that way. It was easier not to care.

That had been until she had laid eyes on Will, and her libido had returned with a vengeance. The universe really had a warped sense of humor. The first genuine interest she had felt since Andre, and it had to be right back here on the same small island in Alaska. Someone who was living in the same house as her. Someone who was technically her employee.

Sarah reminded herself that she had a strict policy not to date people she worked with. She'd been tempted to bypass it more than once. She spent a lot of time with her clients, often in dimly lit restaurants over several glasses, sometimes bottles, of wine. But when there had been any mutual attraction, Sarah hadn't acted on it until after their contract had been signed and completed.

Things were no different now.

Footsteps on the stairs brought her back to the moment. Personal dilemma aside, she was no closer to having dinner on the table.

Will joined her in the kitchen. "Anything I can help with?"

She quirked an eyebrow at him. "How do you feel about meeting the locals?"

Will cocked his head to the side. "Meeting the locals?"

Sarah grabbed the truck keys and gestured for him to follow her. "Come on. We're going to the Buck."

Will pointed to the dog at his feet. "What about Bart? Should I leave him inside? I can put him in my room."

Sarah lifted a shoulder. "Bring him."

He wrinkled his forehead. "You sure?"

She grinned. "Welcome to Alaska."

CHAPTER NINE

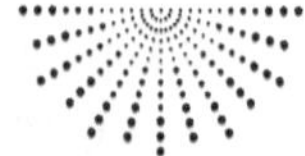

SARAH

Will opened the door for Sarah. She thanked him and walked into the bar, taking a deep breath of stale beer, fried food, and lemon cleaner mixed together. Sarah smiled. It smelled like home.

A gravelly voice called out from behind the bar. "I know that can't be Sarah Carter standing in my restaurant."

Sarah's heart squeezed at the familiar voice. "Hey Wolfie. I'm back."

He smiled. "I heard."

Of course he had heard. There were no secrets in this small town. It was part of the reason she had left.

Sarah pointed at Bart. "Mind if we take a booth? We have this guy with us."

Wolfie gestured to the far wall. "You help yourself. I'll be over in a minute with a couple."

Sarah crossed the bar to a booth with a window seat. The street was lit with the last bit of daylight, softening the faded paint and rough exterior of the few other buildings in town.

Darling looked kind of nice, or would have, if Sarah hadn't known what living here was really like.

Will slipped into the bench seat across from her, placing Bart on the floor. The dog's wiry form disappeared under the table. "What did he mean? A couple of what?"

Two pint classes appeared in front of them. "A couple of beers. I know you two didn't come here for my company. I'm Wolfie."

Wolfie smiled, his blue eyes bright beneath bushy gray brows that matched his styled mustache.

Will reached out and shook Wolfie's hand. "Will. Nice to meet you. I'm going to be working at the lodge for the summer."

"Nice to meet you, too. The rest of that isn't news." Wolfie smoothed his beard, glancing at Sarah. "Your brother was in here earlier, yelling his head off about it. I sent him home with a growler, so he is either feeling better by now, or he's asleep."

"I thought family was supposed to support you," Sarah grumbled as she reached for her beer. It was one thing for Mac to disagree with her. But did he have to tell the whole damn town?

She took a sip of her drink, the familiar yeasty flavor making her feel ten times better. She smiled. "You really know how to turn a mood around. If Mac isn't feeling better after having some of this, then I'm not sure he's human."

"I'll leave you to your therapy." Wolfie winked. "Back in a minute."

Sarah took a second sip, closing her eyes for a moment. When she had told her parents she'd hired Will for the summer, they had seemed fine with it. She was even paying him out of her own savings. But when it came to Mac, she couldn't do anything right.

"You okay?" Will asked.

Sarah blinked her eyes open. Will was another problem. She'd hired him to help her, not to distract her. "Just fine. How do you like the beer?"

He held up his half-empty glass. "I'll let you decide."

She smiled. "You should tell Wolfie. He knows it's good, but he can't hear it enough. He makes it himself, so it's a point of pride for him. Trust Germans with beer."

Will snapped his fingers. "That's where he's from!"

Sarah nodded. "You're going to have to ask him about that story one day. The only hint I'm giving you is that it's not boring."

Wolfie came up to their table again to take their orders. They were the only two in the place at such an odd hour, and their food was delivered quickly.

Sarah scooped up her chili, piled high with chopped onions and melted cheddar cheese. The spices made her nose tingle, and her stomach growled appreciatively at the first bite.

Will bit into a golden onion ring with a crunch and let out a moan. "This meal would be eighty bucks in Seattle."

"Same for LA," she agreed. "And that would be a bargain."

"Do you miss it?" he asked as he picked up his burger.

Sarah swallowed and reached for her beer as she debated how much to share. All Will really needed to know was that she needed help with the lodge this summer. As far as why she had left in the first place? That wasn't important. "I do. My entire life was in LA. Trust me, a week here and you will cry for Seattle. I'm bracing myself for when you decide to break your contract early and head back."

Will shook his head, his eyes turned down. "I don't think you have a lot to worry about. Things back there, well, I'll just say it was time to leave."

"So you aren't going back?"

He wiped his hands on a napkin. "I'll have to see what things look like at the end of summer."

Sarah nodded slowly. Will hadn't told her much about his own life, either. All she knew was that he had a lot of experience doing the work the lodge needed, and that he was willing to come to Alaska at the last minute. And it was all she needed to know.

"So you've never been to Europe." Will changed the subject as he slipped Bart a fry.

The hair on the back of Sarah's neck stood up. He had remembered what she had said about not going to Europe. She had to be careful with this one—he listened. "No, but I would love to go one day. Have you been?"

"I have. But we're talking about you. Why don't you go?"

Sarah set her spoon in the empty bowl and pushed it away. "I don't know. I think it would be more fun to travel with somebody, for one."

He cocked his head to the side. "There's no one in LA you would want to go with? A friend? A boyfriend?"

She shifted in her seat. If she didn't know better, she would have guessed Will was fishing about her relationship status. "There's no one. And I doubt there will be anytime soon."

Will held her gaze. "You never know."

A shiver traveled down her back and solidified what she already knew: She was doomed.

Wolfie came to her rescue, collecting their empty dishes and swapping out the plates for a bottle of clear liquid. "I know you have to drive back to the lodge, so take this to go."

Sarah held up the bottle and peered through the glass. "This isn't what I think it is, is it?"

Wolfie grinned. "It's exactly what you think it is."

She shuddered. "Then I am definitely drinking this at home."

Once Wolfie left, Sarah stood, gesturing for Will to get up. "Come on, we have to move fast."

She peeled off a couple of bills and set them on the table before making a beeline for the door.

Will caught up to her. "But he didn't even bring the check."

"He won't." Sarah whispered. "The stubborn old man won't take any money. Not sure how this place stays in business. We all just leave what we feel is right, probably more than right, and it covers the people who can't leave anything. Sometimes the only thing that protects you from the dark up here is a warm meal and time with people you care about."

Sarah placed her hand on the door handle when she heard Wolfie's call after her.

"See you next time, Sarah."

She turned to see him watching her from behind the bar. His eyes searched her face, and she reached up to touch her chin. "What is it? Do I have something on my face?"

He smiled and shook his head. "It's just nice to see you with someone again. Almost reminds me of…"

"Good bye," she cut Wolfie off and turned on her heel as her body broke out into a cold sweat. She walked out of the Buck so fast she was dizzy by the time she got to the truck.

Will trailed behind her. "What's going on? You okay?"

Sarah pressed her lips together, opened the door, and climbed into the cab. She didn't want to talk about it because she didn't want to remember. And the last person who needed to know anything about her past was Will.

She knew what everyone in Darling thought. They felt bad for her. Poor Sarah, all alone. But no one knew the truth. And the truth was that she didn't deserve to be with someone again, not after what she had done.

Sarah shoved the schnapps between the seat cushions.

Now she just had to get home so she could drink it. Maybe, just maybe, that would help her forget everything she could never have.

CHAPTER TEN

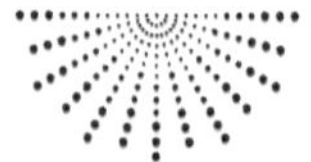

WILL

Something wet touched Will's face. Something wet and stinky. With a groan, he rolled over and covered his head with a pillow, dodging Bart's next lick. He wanted to tell his dog to leave him alone, but he couldn't get the words out. Not with his tongue cemented to the top of his mouth.

Sarah had been right. The schnapps was no joke. She'd warned him again as he'd poured his third glass, but Will had shrugged it off. The drink had been smooth and delicious and it had made him feel happy. There was no way it could be that bad, right?

The vice grip tightened around Will's head. He pried one eye open only to see another gray sky. Same as yesterday. Same as back home.

The ride back from town last night had been quiet. When they'd gotten home and Sarah had offered him a drink, Will had gladly accepted. He could tolerate the tension, but that didn't mean he liked it. And the schnapps had worked its magic, draining the stress from his body.

Sarah had relaxed after a while, and they'd fallen back into casual conversation. She'd talked about the island, the lodge, and asked him questions about Seattle. It was what she hadn't said that had been more interesting to Will. Sarah hadn't shared one personal detail.

Bart whined, and Will knew he had to get out of bed. Bart needed to go out, and Sarah had promised a tour of the island today. He didn't want to start his first full day at the lodge by skipping out. It wouldn't exactly be a great first impression.

He put one foot on the ground and then the other. He hated himself. Will wasn't a college kid anymore, and he sure as heck couldn't drink like one. He'd drunk himself to a hangover after Rachel had told him about the wedding, and he'd done it again on his first night in Darling. He didn't like the pattern.

Will checked the time, and his stomach dropped. It was late. He hoped Sarah hadn't sat around waiting for him. It wasn't like him to sleep for so long, but it also wasn't like him to get plastered on homemade hooch. So far, coming to Alaska didn't seem like his best idea.

He decided on a hot shower before anything else. Maybe that would make him feel better.

Grabbing his towel and toiletry kit, Will headed to the bathroom. He opened up the door only to freeze on the spot.

Sarah was standing in front of the sink.

Naked.

He stood frozen.

"Oh my God!" she screamed and scrambled for a towel. "Close your eyes!"

Will slapped his hand over his face a little too hard, recoiling at the sting. A wave of nausea passed through him.

"What the hell?" she snapped. "Okay, you can look."

He dropped his hand, and found that she had wrapped a

towel around herself in that mysterious way women do, tucked under her arms and somehow staying put.

Sarah scowled at him. "You don't knock first?"

"You don't lock the door?"

Her eyes shot daggers. "I've been here by myself, okay? Besides, I feel like the door being closed made it pretty obvious. That's what doors are for. You can be damn sure I'll lock it from now on!"

Will cringed. So much for a good first impression. "I'm sorry, I'm hungover and—"

"You don't think I'm hungover?"

He furrowed his brow. "But you barely had any of the schnapps."

Sarah rubbed her forehead. "That stuff is lethal, even a little bit of it. Every time I drink it, I wonder why I bother."

Will pressed his lips together, trying not to laugh. So far, he didn't think this morning could be off to a worse start. They were both in fine form.

He turned to leave. "Again, I'm sorry. I'll be in my room. Let me know when you're done."

"Still want to go on that boat ride?"

Will's stomach turned over. "God, no."

Sarah laughed. "I thought as much. We'll figure out something else."

He left the bathroom, and closed the door behind him. Then he took a deep breath. He'd thought he'd been attracted to Sarah before. Now he knew he was. He had never seen a more gorgeous woman in his life.

Not that anything was going to happen between them. He definitely didn't want to get involved with someone he worked for and lived with. It was a recipe for disaster.

Will reached up to massage his throbbing forehead. He had only been here two days.

How had things already gotten so complicated?

* * *

FRESHLY SHOWERED, Will headed downstairs. He felt somewhat human again, but definitely nowhere near good enough to go bobbing around in the water. He was thankful Sarah had taken that off the schedule for today. Bart trotted at his heels, the only one in the house without a hangover. Will was jealous of the dog.

Sarah had a cup of strong coffee waiting for him. She held up an expensive bottle of whiskey. "Hair of the dog?"

He eyed the liquor, his mouth turning sour. "Does that work? I've never been a believer."

She lifted a shoulder. "I'll let you know. So far, so good."

With a grimace, Will took the bottle and added a splash to his mug. The smell made him gag, but after a couple of small sips, he did feel slightly better. He could actually take a deep breath without wanting to yak.

Sarah sipped her coffee. "Okay, no boat ride. Not today. What about that hike?"

Will shuddered. "God, I am so sorry. I swear, I don't normally drink this much. I think my major accomplishment for today will be existing."

She laughed. "How do you feel about a big, greasy breakfast? I'm not much of a cook if last night didn't give that away, but I definitely know how to cure a hangover."

His stomach lurched at the mention of food, but he was willing to try anything. So far, his first morning in Alaska wasn't off to a great start, and he was determined to turn that around. "Food sounds good."

"Sit." Sarah directed him to one of the bar stools that flanked the kitchen island. "And pay attention. This is the most cooking you'll ever see me do."

He watched her move around the kitchen, gathering ingredients from the fridge and cupboards. She grabbed a cast-iron skillet and let it heat for a few minutes before adding strips of bacon that sizzled as soon as they touched the pan.

Bart sniffed the air and let out a whine from where he lay at her feet.

"I promise, there will be some left for you," Sarah cooed.

While the bacon cooked, she cracked half a dozen eggs that she then scrambled in frothy butter and topped with shredded cheese.

She plated the eggs, turned the bacon, and added several slices of bread to the toaster. A few minutes later, they popped up with a beep, just in time to drain the bacon.

Watching Sarah fix breakfast, Will's mind wandered. Blame it on the hangover, but for a few brief seconds, he could almost pretend that this was his life. That maybe he didn't have a storage unit and a failed marriage back in Seattle. Maybe instead he lived in Alaska with a beautiful woman who made him breakfast.

A strange feeling crawled down his back, and he shivered. This was temporary. It wasn't real life.

Sarah put a filled plate in front of Will. "Put honey on your toast. Honey and lots of butter. Works every time. The ultimate hangover cure."

She broke apart a small strip of bacon and set it on a plate on the floor in front of Bart, who gobbled it up with a wag of his skinny tail.

Will reached for the butter and added two thick pats to his toast before drizzling honey over the top. He shoved half the slice in his mouth, and let out a moan of pleasure. It tasted like heaven.

He couldn't remember the last time he'd had a home cooked meal like this. No wonder he had trouble keeping the weight on. He'd spent days surviving on nothing but black coffee. Between dinner at the Buck last night and breakfast this morning, he had a feeling that wouldn't be a problem here.

Will popped the last bit of crust into his mouth before picking up his fork and scooping up a bite of eggs.

Sarah refilled his coffee, adding a second splash of whiskey. "Better?"

He nodded. "Much better. I don't know why you say you're not much of a cook."

She chuckled. "All this should tell you is how many times I've had a hangover. Besides, breakfast is simple. The most complicated thing is the bread, but I grabbed that loaf from the freezer."

"It's homemade? I don't know anyone who makes their own sourdough."

Sarah cleared away the breakfast dishes, setting them in the sink. "I also bet you don't know many people who take a boat to the dentist. What I did today wasn't special. It's just how people do things here."

After Will cleaned his plate, he felt like a new man. He helped Sarah load the dishwasher and then wiped down the kitchen counters. "Okay, I think I'm going to live."

She peered at him. "We should play it safe. How do you feel about going into town?"

He held up a finger. "Under one condition."

"What's that?" she asked.

"I don't want to go to the Buck."

Sarah grinned. "Now you're sounding like a local."

CHAPTER ELEVEN

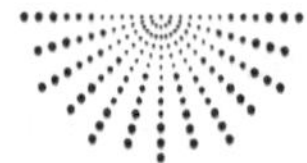

WILL

Unable to convince Bart to get up from his post-bacon nap, Will made sure the dog had plenty of food and water before he joined Sarah in the truck.

"He won't even know we're gone," Sarah reassured Will as he watched the lodge disappear behind them.

"It's not Bart I'm worried about."

"No one is going to bother the lodge. People don't even lock their cars out here. Plus, the eagles haven't figured out how to work the door handle yet." She winked at him.

He gave a small smile. On a logical level, Will knew Sarah was the expert on this place, not him. But his cautious nature struggled to release control. He took a deep breath and told himself to enjoy the ride.

They bounced along in the truck, with an old rock cassette as their soundtrack. There was no AC, no automatic windows, and the doors had almost rusted shut. Sarah joked the vehicle had an Alaskan body.

The gravel road made for a rough ride, and Will rolled the

window down halfway. The cool air blowing in his face soothed his nausea.

The road opened up, and the trees stood further back from the road to make way for weathered wood structures in faded colors. More than one of them appeared to be empty. Further down the street, sat another group of what looked like houses. At one point, there must have been an actual town here.

Sarah pulled the truck over in front of a beige building and put it into park. "Mind if we run inside and grab a few things? Then I can give you the grand tour. Which will take all of five minutes."

"Sounds good." Will stepped tentatively out of the truck. Thank God she'd made him eat something before they'd left. The only thing worse than getting drunk on his first night here would be to throw up in front of everyone in broad daylight. This definitely wasn't his finest hour.

He followed her into the building, and a bell sounded over the door when they entered.

"Hello?" Sarah called out.

"Be right out!" a woman's voice came from the back.

Will glanced around. Household goods, groceries, and various supplies sat together in an orderly fashion. With the light just right, he could see a fine layer of dust on just about everything. The place had a slightly musty smell, and looked more like a museum than a functioning business. Paired with the bell over the door, it felt like they had time traveled to the past.

A woman poked her head out of the back of the store. Eyes wide, she ran over to Sarah, and wrapped gangly arms around her. "It's you!"

Sarah giggled. "I missed you too, Viv."

The woman stepped back, her hands resting on Sarah's arms. "I didn't think you'd ever come back."

Sarah's face grew tight, and suddenly she looked ten years older than he knew her to be. He frowned as he looked between the two women. Had he missed something? "Of course I came back."

The woman's eyebrows knitted together. "But after what happened…"

"A long time ago," Sarah interrupted. "Let me introduce you to Will."

Will reached out his hand. It was obvious Sarah had wanted to change the subject, but that only made him more curious. Why had this woman thought Sarah would never come back? Something serious must have happened. Something Sarah hadn't told Will.

"Will Brooks, nice to meet you. I'm the new handyman at the lodge."

The woman shook his hand. "Vivian Locke. My parents own the store." She released her grip and crossed her arms. "How long are you in town for?"

"Just the summer."

Vivian pursed her lips and glanced at Sarah. It seemed Will wasn't the only one who didn't have a clue what was going on.

Sarah clasped her hands together, rocking back on her heels. "Anyway, we're just going to grab a few things and head back to the lodge. We won't bother you much longer."

Will waited silently while Sarah picked out what she needed, her hands unsteady as she plucked items from the shelves. Then he helped her carry everything to the truck.

Sarah slammed the tailgate shut, her mouth a thin line.

Will cleared his throat. "Hey. Are you okay?"

She smiled at him, but it didn't quite reach her eyes. "I'm fine. How about that tour?"

Will followed her down the wooden walkway. Whatever

had happened back there, she clearly didn't want to talk about it. It wasn't like he had any right to pry.

"You know the Buck and the store now. There's also the ferry terminal, though it's really just a dock. Mac's shop is that way." Sarah pointed down the street, if the dirt and gravel path that led through town qualified as a street.

Will looked up and down the row of buildings. "So where are the tourists? Do they come on cruise ships?"

Sarah shook her head. "Darling doesn't have a deep enough dock. We get the people trying to get away from the cruise ship traffic. Believe it or not, it started with Mac's flight business. He used to only help the locals make plane connections and pick up orders in Juneau. Stuff like that. One day, someone from San Francisco called up and wanted Mac to take him and his wife sightseeing by air. Flightseeing, that's what they call it. I just about fainted when I heard how much they were paying."

Will chuckled. The most unbelievable part was that Mac hadn't scared off every potential customer. "And those people stay at the lodge?"

Sarah kicked at the ground, leaving a scuff in the packed dirt."Yep."

"What about all these buildings? What are they?"

"Those over there are houses," she said, confirming his earlier guess. "And these," she gestured to the buildings around them, "are all broken dreams."

Sarah's shoulders hunched as she peered into the window of one of the empty buildings. "I think this used to be a pizza parlor. There was also a clothing store, a medical clinic, and an outdoor supply shop. But that's what this place does, you know? Takes what you care about and gives nothing back. Only you don't realize it until you're left grasping empty air."

Goosebumps rose on his arms. Sarah had scars. Whatever

had happened had hurt her deeply. Her broken dream must have been more than a failed business venture, but what?

He shoved his hands in his pockets, struggling for something to say. "I don't know, doesn't seem that bad."

She turned towards him. "You think I'm being dramatic. Talk to me in a few months."

Will was going to tell her he had the advantage of having nothing left in Seattle. He'd already lost his wife, his company, and his best friend. If what she said was true, well, there was nothing else to take from him.

But he didn't get the chance to say any of that before Sarah grabbed Will's jacket and pulled him around the corner of a building.

"Shit." She reached her arm across his body, flattening both of them against the wall. They were so close he could see the flecks of brown and gold in her green eyes. The faint freckles on her nose.

He was a sucker for freckles.

Will opened his mouth to ask her what was wrong, but she placed a finger on his lips and shook her head. Could she feel the surge of heat that ran down his body? He hoped not. Not that he could control it even if he'd tried.

How long would they stay here? An older woman crossed the street. Will felt her gaze on them for just a moment before she kept walking.

Several minutes passed before Sarah's body relaxed, and she moved away from Will. She seemed to be looking everywhere but at him. "I'm so sorry. I'm just not ready for some people yet. It's this place; it does weird things to you. But I can't hide forever, right?"

Will hesitated. Was she expecting an answer? Based on recent experience, he was far from qualified to give life advice. "Are you sure you're okay?"

She gave him a tight smile. "Never better. Ready to head

back?" Without waiting for him to respond, she headed in the direction of the truck.

Will fell into step behind her.

I can't hide forever.

What exactly was she hiding from?

But even if he asked, Will had a feeling that question would go unanswered like so many others had. Will had come to Alaska to get away from a complicated situation, not to instantly get into another one. It should scare him off, but instead it only made him want to get closer to her.

Could he trust himself at all?

CHAPTER TWELVE

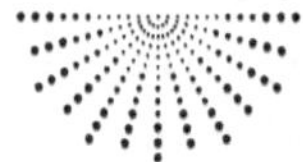

SARAH

Sarah checked the calendar, and rubbed the bridge of her nose. Monday. That wasn't a surprise. Only a Monday could be this awful.

She'd struggled with balancing the books since she'd poured her first cup of coffee that morning. Now they were two hours past lunch, and she still hadn't figured out the math.

She'd avoided this particular pile of paperwork since she'd arrived in Alaska, but there was no way around it anymore. With reservations coming in and expenses for improvements on the lodge going out, she needed to know what numbers they were working with.

She let down her ponytail and shook out her hair, but the headache remained.

She couldn't figure it out. Her parents had grown up with money. They were academics, the definition of intelligent people. They had kept this place running for almost three decades, so why did everything point to the fact that they were flat broke?

Her mind wandered to her own bank account balance. It had taken a hit from her time here, but was still reasonably healthy. But she needed that money to pay Will, not to mention to start her life over.

Again.

With a sigh, she leaned back in the desk chair. Bart whimpered, and Sarah reached down to scratch his ears. He should have had a bald patch from all the times she'd treated him as her personal therapy dog. He still slept in Will's room at night, but he spent his days inside the lodge with her.

The sounds of a swinging hammer rang through the air. Will had been working on the front porch day and night since his first infamous day here. Sarah had told him she didn't expect miracles, and that neither did the regulars. But Will worked like a man possessed, keeping himself busy almost the entire day. Which was good, because Will was another problem she hadn't been able to solve.

Her phone dinged. Sarah reached for it, frowning at the screen. It was another text from Aaron, asking her if everything was okay. He really was a sweet guy, but getting involved with him had been a mistake. Aaron deserved better. Just because relationships weren't for her didn't mean other people felt the same way.

This time, Sarah had every intention of sticking to her no dating at work rule. But with Will in the picture, that was easier said than done. Being back home should have been the ultimate mood killer. Instead, this place did strange things to her. Like making her wonder what all that handyman work did to his abs.

As she tapped out a reply to Aaron, the hammering ceased. The silence was followed by the sound of footsteps on the front porch.

A light knock came at the door, and her stomach did a somersault.

Sarah cleared her throat, tucking a strand of hair behind her ear. She needed to get a grip. "Come in."

Will smiled as he stepped into the office. "I'm going to get a glass of lemonade. Want one?"

Sarah glanced at the desk. She had sat in this chair and worked until her butt had gone numb, but the pile of paperwork only seemed to grow larger. Maybe a break would help. She scooped Bart up as she stood. "Okay. But I want vodka in mine."

Will laughed, and her stomach did another gymnastic move. It really wasn't fair that he was so attractive. "I take it the accounting is going well?"

Sarah blew air through her lips as she followed Will to the kitchen. "At this point, I'm tempted to lean on the keyboard and hope for the best. My parents always handled this stuff, and now I know why. What a nightmare."

He tipped the pitcher over a tall glass and handed it to her. "Why don't you just go over and ask them?"

Sarah sniffed the glass. "Maybe if you had given me vodka."

Will leaned against the counter, his shirt taut against his flat stomach. Sarah took a gulp of lemonade. "You seriously think they're avoiding you?"

She set down the glass and gave him a look. "We walk by their cabin every night when we take Bart out. Half the time my mom is sleeping. The other half, they're happier to see Bart than me."

Will chuckled and gestured to the snoring dog. "Can you blame them? Okay, so you don't want to ask your parents. Then let's go with plan B. Doing something fun."

Sarah knit her brows together. "Fun?"

"Fun," Will repeated. "Have you heard of it? You've been working all day, every day. Maybe you're just burned out."

Sarah sighed. If only he knew she hadn't just done it this way since she got to Alaska. She'd been doing it for years. She wasn't sure if she even remembered how to have fun anymore. "That would help if there was something to do around here."

He took a sip of his drink. "I'm sure we can think of something. What did you do as a kid?"

Sarah bit her lip. She had spent the past five years trying to forget every memory she'd made in Alaska. It felt weird trying to remember them. But there had been good memories too, hadn't there? "Okay, here's something. There's this house at the north end of the island that has a big rope swing down on the beach. All the kids loved that thing. It didn't even matter if the water was freezing. Sometimes, two or three of us would swing at once. You can guess how much our parents loved that."

"Think you're too old for that?" Will asked with a wink.

Sarah's face heated up. She could do without the frigid water, but she wouldn't mind seeing Will in a pair of swim shorts. Not that she should be fantasizing about Will at all. "Doesn't matter. No one has lived in that house for years. The rope would probably disintegrate the minute you touched it."

He set down his empty glass. "Too bad. Maybe someday someone will spruce the place up, and you can show me how it's done. I personally have never willingly jumped into a freezing ocean."

She laughed. "Hey, I was a kid. I'm not sure I would do it now either."

Will grinned. "Maybe we can do it together. You said you used to go two at a time, right?"

Sarah swallowed. She reminded herself that all of this was temporary. Doing dishes together, the evening walks, talking about their day. It would come to an end. But none of that stopped her heart from whispering its dangerous ideas.

Because what if it didn't?

Flustered, she chugged the rest of her drink and set the empty glass in the sink. "I should probably get back. I have a pile of paperwork waiting for me."

Before Will could say anything, she scurried off to the office and closed the door behind her. She took a deep breath. She was freaking out about nothing. Even if she did like Will, that didn't mean he felt the same way.

Sarah forced herself to return to the mountain of paperwork her parents considered their accounting system. Her stomach twisted with guilt.

Maybe Mac was right. Was it true that when Sarah made a decision, everyone paid for it? She had stayed away too long and look what happened? Her mom had gotten hurt, and the lodge was falling apart.

She needed to fix the mess she'd made. The last thing she needed was the complications of a crush. She'd have to be crazy to think that was a good idea. After all, if life had taught her anything, it's that she wasn't meant for a relationship.

Her cell phone rang, the blaring ringtone startling her. She had picked the awful sound on purpose, never wanting to miss a work call.

The instant she saw her boss's name on the Caller ID, she felt wide awake.

"Hello?"

"Sarah, it's Desirae."

From the background noise it sounded like her boss was driving. That was a good sign, right? People didn't multitask when they had bad news, did they? "Desirae, hi. How are you? How's LA?"

"I should be asking you how Alaska is." Desirae cleared her throat. "Sorry I never answered your email, is now a good time to talk?"

A sense of dread seeped through her body, and Sarah's stomach sank. She checked to make sure she was sitting down. She had the feeling she should be. "Yeah, sure."

Desirae sighed. "Look, I'm not going to beat around the bush. I thought about it. It's been a couple of weeks. I need someone here, so I filled your position. I wish I could've kept it open for you, but you remember I didn't promise anything, right? I'll take care of all the paperwork, cash out any time on the books you have left. If you ever come back down here, you let me know, okay?"

Sarah felt dizzy. "Okay."

The call ended, and she set the phone on the desk.

Resting her head in her hands, Sarah tried to make sense of it. But no matter how she did the math, she came up with the same answer—she didn't have a job waiting for her in Los Angeles.

How would she pay for her condo when she got back? Should she even keep it? And that was assuming she went back at all.

What if she was stuck here forever?

Her throat grew tight, and the room closed in around her. This place was too small. Suddenly she needed to be anywhere but here. She stood up, and before she knew it, she was running, running, running.

The ground beneath her changed from wood to dirt, and tiny rocks stabbed at the soles of her feet. The dark forest passed by in a blurry shadow. A layer of mist coated her face, wet and cold.

A voice called after her, but Sarah kept moving. She had to get away! She couldn't get away.

There was only one problem with trying to run away on an island—eventually, there was only water.

Sarah toppled off the dock and hit the freezing ocean with a splash.

CHAPTER THIRTEEN

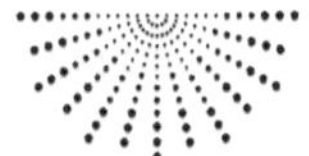

SARAH

Sarah had spent countless hours in the ocean growing up. She and Mac had used to swim through the shallows, slick as otters while they'd collected sea asparagus in the clear, cold water.

But she'd never been afraid in the water.

Until tonight.

She struggled with the urge to breathe, panicking as she tried to figure out which way was up. She reached out to grip the small dock, but her hand only sliced through the water. Her clothes became heavy, pulling her down as they soaked through.

She used to think she was a strong swimmer. What else could she be if this had been her swimming pool? But in California, she had rarely done more than dip her toes in the ocean the few days she'd found time to go to the beach. Not to mention that her cardio workouts had consisted of running from meeting to meeting. None of which served her now.

The collar of her shirt tightened around her throat, cutting off what little oxygen she sucked in between ragged breaths. A hand clamped around her arm and dragged her out of the water. Her clothes caught on the dock, and the wood scraped her bare skin.

She found herself on her hands and knees, gasping as she faced the rough wood planks. Finally catching her breath, Sarah rubbed her neck and then straightened on her knees to pull her shirt down.

Will stood in front of her.

"You," she breathed.

"Are you okay?" he asked, clasping her hand and helping her to her feet. Patches of wet covered his clothes. "What the hell happened?"

Sarah shook her head. "You don't want to know. It's stupid. I'm stupid."

Will placed his warm hands on her shoulders. "You're not stupid. Tell me, please. I just rescued someone from drowning; I'm curious."

He gave her shoulders a squeeze, and Sarah's gaze traveled up his arms. Arms that strained against his shirt sleeves. Arms that had saved her.

Her stomach turned over. With a groan, Sarah dropped her head in her hands. This must be some sort of psychological phenomenon. There was no way that she had almost drowned minutes ago, and now all she could think about was how sexy her rescuer was.

"Sarah, what's wrong?"

She looked up to see his eyes searching her face. She went with the least embarrassing revelation. "I don't have a job in Los Angeles anymore."

Will raised an eyebrow. "Are you seriously telling me you threw yourself off the dock because of a stupid job?"

She rubbed her arms. "I didn't mean to throw myself off.

God, you don't have to make this sound like some kind of dramatic Victorian romance novel. I panicked and left the lodge. I misjudged how long the dock was, okay?"

Will massaged his temples. "Don't do it again. There are a ton of jobs out there. In the meantime, I am sure your parents would be happy to have you right here. Either way, it's not worth sinking to the bottom of the ocean for."

"Did it ever occur to you that I don't want to be right here? That I want to be anywhere else but here?" Her voice cracked, and she pressed her lips together.

Will gestured around them. "Why? This place is perfect. Safe. Gorgeous. Nice people. Seems like the perfect place to raise a family. Build a life."

Sarah snorted. "Everyone's dream."

His eyes narrowed. "What's your problem?"

She clenched her fists to keep her hands from shaking. "My problem is that you know nothing about this place. You came here for the summer like every other tourist. You don't know how hard it is. Stay a few winters. Survive people putting your personal life under a microscope. Tell me how easy it is to raise a family when the person you love..." She looked away.

"What?" he asked softly, pushing the wet strands of hair away from her face.

Her eyes burned. She knew the action meant nothing. But his touch unlocked something deep inside her, like blowing the dust off of a long-forgotten book.

Suddenly she remembered things that were better left in the past. Memories from another life, of another man who cared about her. What it felt like to be loved, really loved.

"Oh God, don't cry. I don't know what to do when women cry," Will begged.

Sarah hiccuped. "I don't know what to do either. I don't

even know why I'm crying. It's stupid," she squeaked as she wiped at her eyes.

Will wrapped his arms around her, and she pushed herself into him, leaning on his hard chest. Like a sunflower to the sun, she soaked up his warmth and the minty smell of him.

She told herself it shouldn't feel this good, that she didn't need this. She wouldn't miss this. But something about this embrace made her forget all the reasons why it shouldn't happen.

Her tears dried up, and her breathing slowed.

"It's going to be okay," Will said.

Without thinking, Sarah tipped her head back and found his mouth.

What was she doing? Her eyes flew open, realizing what she had done. She pulled away, but Will's arms only tightened around her, bringing her closer as he kissed her back.

Her eyes closed, and she melted into him. She didn't know how much time passed while she let Will kiss away every ounce of pain she felt, warming her to the tips of her toes.

"Sarah." His voice was husky as he pulled away. "We have to get you changed out of these clothes."

"Is that a move?" She teased, hoping he would say yes.

"No." He smiled warmly, his eyes crinkling at the corners. "I'm a fan of the idea, trust me, but this isn't the time. I'll make you a deal, how about you get changed while I clean up from lunch?"

Sarah nodded and took Will's hand as he led her back to the lodge.

By the time she'd taken a hot shower and had changed into dry clothes, Will had cleaned up the kitchen. She'd noticed he was like that—if he said he was going to do something, he did it.

Will handed her a steaming mug. "Feel better?"

Sarah peered into the cup. "I'm in the mood for something a little stronger than tea."

"There is whiskey in it." Will winked.

She grinned. "I knew I liked you for a reason."

Together, they made their way to the living room, where they settled on the overstuffed sofa. Only half of a couch cushion separated them. Sarah was as aware of the heat radiating from the teacup, as she was of Will's body.

"All we're missing is a fire," she mused, gazing up at the river rock fireplace that reached to the ceiling. She looked back at Will. "That is the only bad thing about summer."

Will lifted his shoulder. "Luckily, I don't know what I'm missing."

"What are you doing after this?" Sarah asked, not sure she wanted to know. "Do you know where you are going yet?"

He frowned at her. "Going?"

"For your next job."

"Oh, right." Will took a sip from his mug. "Not yet. Besides, we have other things to talk about. You just had a near death experience, remember? Or have you blocked it out already?"

Sarah dunked her tea bag, trying to focus on something besides her feelings and his blue eyes. "It's this place. It does things to people. I can't stay here. I can't do this again."

"Is this the part where you tell me what you're talking about?"

She sighed and sunk further into the couch. "You don't want to hear it. It's boring."

"Nothing about you is boring."

Sarah glanced at Will's mouth, and her mind jumped back to their kiss on the dock. Heat churned in her belly, and she hated herself. Hated herself for hating this place, and missing Andre, and somehow still having feelings for Will. Hated herself for not having learned her lesson the first time around.

Her heart pounded in her chest. After having spent years trying not to think about what had happened, it terrified her to speak it out loud. "I grew up with the love of my life on this island."

"Definitely not boring," Will said in an even tone.

Sarah licked her lips. It would be so easy to stop there. But she wanted Will to understand. Once he knew the truth, there wouldn't be any chance of something happening between them. She was saving them both from pain. "I was a goner from the moment I met him. It's such a cliche, but it really was love at first sight."

Will rested his chin on his fist. "I take it he felt the same way."

Sarah twisted a strand of damp hair, the water droplets leaving tiny dark spots on her jeans. "He did. As far as we were concerned, there was no one else. I remember thinking how lucky we were that we found each other, that we grew up on the same island, of all the places on earth."

Will lifted a corner of his mouth. "Sounds like a real love story."

Sarah rested her palm in her lap, turning it up to look at the lines there. Natasha had read her palm once, a long time ago. She'd gotten the feeling she hadn't told her everything she'd seen, and Sarah had always wondered if it had had something to do with what had happened to Andre. "It was a love story. Right up until he disappeared."

Will shifted in his seat. "Disappeared?"

She nodded slowly. "Went off in his boat one day and never came back."

"They never found him? Not even a clue?"

Sarah took a sip from her cup, and the whiskey burned down her throat. "Not a thing. After that, all I cared about was leaving this place. Everything around here, every person, just reminded me that he was gone."

She set her cup aside. She was on the edge of crying again, her chest growing tight as sweat prickled her underarms. She needed to calm down and tell Will everything.

The only problem was she had told no one before. She could barely admit it to herself.

Sarah looked up and locked eyes with Will. She had his attention—she only needed courage.

Bart let out a yip, and they both looked up in time to see a raven fly away from its perch in the spruce tree outside the window.

Whatever bubble they'd been in burst. Sarah blinked, almost surprised to find they were still in the lodge, that it was still daylight.

Will covered her hand with his. "Are you okay?"

"Fine." She snatched her hand away and stood. "Thanks for the tea. And you know, saving my life."

He lifted one corner of his mouth. "Anytime."

Sarah walked quickly to her office and closed the door behind her. For a moment, she was back in another time, another place.

Everything she'd told Will about Andre had been true. But it hadn't been a love story. Because only one of them had been in love.

CHAPTER FOURTEEN

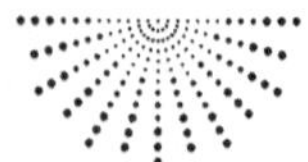

WILL

"Nice to see you again," Sarah's dad grinned as he pumped Will's hand up and down.

Will smiled back. "Same here."

Sarah's mom limped through the front door. "We've been looking forward to this all day."

"Let me help you with that." Will lent her his arm as he guided her to a seat at the kitchen table.

Sarah had told him her parents were coming over for dinner but that he didn't have to stick around if he didn't want to. She'd offered him a ride to the Buck if he'd wanted an out. "But no promises on a ride back. I have a feeling this night won't end with me sober."

Will had declined the ride and stayed. He figured Sarah could use an extra hand.

"This place looks wonderful," Sarah's mom said.

"It certainly does." Sarah's dad looked at Will. "I don't think the front porch has looked that nice since they built it. You're pretty good at that kind of stuff."

Will shrugged. "A lifetime of practice."

Though most of that time he'd spent running a multi-million dollar company, not actually constructing.

"Hello, Bart." Sarah's mom greeted the dog with a pat on his head.

"You know, I don't know why we never got a dog. I quite like this little guy." She threw a sidelong glance toward the kitchen. "It's as close as we'll ever get to grandkids."

"Mac is also fully capable of having kids," Sarah yelled from where she was rushing around, putting the last minute touches on dinner.

Will swallowed. He and Sarah hadn't talked about kids. But why would they? It wasn't like they were going to get married. Besides, if Will was ever brave enough to trade vows with someone again, he wanted to be certain it was someone who wanted the same things as him. And that included kids.

He shook off Sarah's comment and joined her in the kitchen. It was pointless to overthink a situation that they both knew was temporary. Will focused on helping with dinner instead. "Need a hand?"

Sarah shook her head and ducked into the pantry, resurfacing with a bottle of red wine. "Care for a glass? It's the good stuff."

Will gave an enthusiastic nod. Maybe a drink would quiet the chatter in his mind. "Yes, please."

Sarah poured three glasses, handing the third to her dad.

"Hey!" her mom protested.

Sarah raised an eyebrow. "I thought it might interact with your pain meds."

Her mom looked away and tugged on the hem of her shirt. "I only take them when I wake up and go to bed. I haven't had one for hours. You know how early I get up. Just one glass."

Sarah turned to her dad, who shrugged. "It won't be the first time, and she's always been fine. Let's just enjoy the evening. It's family dinner."

"Speaking of, where's Maverick?" Sarah's mom asked.

Will glared at Sarah, who suddenly became very occupied with bringing the food to the table. Her invitation to shuttle him off to the Buck made more sense now. He followed her into the kitchen. "I didn't know Mac was coming."

"You didn't?" Sarah squeaked. "I'm sorry. I thought I told you."

Will had only had a sip of wine. He could still drive to town. But the thump of heavy boots on the porch let him know it was already too late. Two short knocks preceded Mac's entrance.

Based on his scowl, Mac hadn't expected Will to be there, either.

"Hi Mom." Mac leaned over to kiss his mom on the cheek and held up a bottle of port. "Picked this up for you in Juneau."

She clapped her hands together. "My favorite!"

Sarah took the bottle from Mac and went to stow it in the kitchen. "So much for one glass," she muttered as she passed Will.

She made her way back to the table where everyone but her and Will already sat. He pulled out an empty chair for her.

Sarah froze, and Will felt three sets of eyes on him. He'd thought he was being polite, why were they acting like he'd just taken off his shirt to wave it over his head while chanting?

"Thank you," Sarah whispered as she sat down.

As they dug into pot roast with gravy, roasted asparagus, and freshly baked rolls, Will listened to Sarah's family as they discussed the weather and what was going on in town. Mac complained about the cruise ship traffic in Juneau for five solid minutes. It was the most Will had ever heard the man talk.

Will helped himself to a second serving of pot roast, mindful of the cherry pie that sat cooling on the kitchen counter. If only Rachel could see him now. He didn't have a problem remembering to eat anymore. "This is delicious, Sarah."

"Thank you." She beamed, and her cheeks turned rosy.

Mac narrowed his eyes, looking between the two of them. He slurped on his wine and turned towards Will. "You don't have someone back home to make you dinner?"

Will shoved a forkful of potato in his mouth and chewed slowly. He'd always prided himself on telling the truth, but he wasn't about to get into the details of his divorce and all the drama that went with it. At least not tonight. "I was in a long-term relationship, but it recently ended. So no, there isn't anyone now."

Their mom shot Mac a scalding look. "We're sorry to hear that, Will. I'm sure Maverick didn't mean to pry."

"Speak for yourself," Mac mumbled into his wine.

Will's gaze connected with Sarah's. He shifted in his seat, uncomfortable at the pity in her eyes. "It's fine. It was for the best."

He glanced at Bart sleeping in his small bed next to the kitchen island. The muscles in Will's back tightened at the memory of Rachel claiming the dog was rightfully hers. What he'd said was the truth—it was for the best.

His phone vibrated in his pocket. Speak of the devil. He didn't need to look to know who it was. There was only one person who called him these days.

He stood from the table and set his empty plate in the farmhouse sink. "Excuse me. I'll be right back."

Bart looked up as Will passed him, but stayed on his bed in the warm kitchen. Will didn't blame him.

Stepping outside, he answered the call. "What do you want, Rachel?"

"I know I taught you better manners than that."

Will cringed. Was this the woman he had been in love with all these years? Either she had changed or he had, because now he dreaded even a simple phone call with her.

"What do you want?" He repeated the question. If she wanted manners, she could get them from her new boyfriend, or fiancé, or whatever Jason was to her now.

She sighed impatiently, as if Will were the one being difficult. "Are you coming to the wedding or not? We are trying to get a head count, and you haven't sent in your RSVP yet. The deadline was two weeks ago. I'm trying to be nice here."

Will stepped away from the lodge, shoulders climbing to his ears. "Nice? Is that what you call cheating on me with my best friend? I'm sorry I didn't RSVP to your wedding. I've been busy getting a divorce."

While she ranted, Will walked further away from the lodge. The last thing he needed was someone walking in on this conversation.

Finally, Rachel ran out of steam, and in their tradition, told Will to go to hell before finishing the call. He stared at the phone and once again wondered what he'd been thinking when he'd married her.

"Good evening," a woman's voice interrupted his thoughts.

Will almost jumped out of his skin. Heart racing, he turned to find an older woman behind him. In the dim light of dusk, the halo of graying hair seemed to float around her head. Blue eyes winked at him, bright and curious, and Will realized it was the woman they had seen in town. There should be nothing scary about an old woman, but then why had Sarah hid from her? "Good evening."

She smiled at him. "I didn't mean to startle you. I'm not used to running into people out here this time of day."

His heart rate began to return to normal. "I think that goes both ways. I wasn't expecting anyone either."

"I'm Natasha. You're Will, right?"

He nodded. "What gave me away?"

She shrugged, her rain jacket crinkling. "Nothing. Just the virtue of living in a small town. No secrets here."

Will smiled, feeling silly that she had scared him. "Good to know."

"I'll let you get back to your evening. Oh, and Will?"

"Yes?"

"You can't judge yourself for the choices you made before. Have some compassion for yourself. Rachel is who she is."

A tingle crawled up his back as he watched Natasha walk away without making a sound on the forest path. No wonder he hadn't heard her. But how did she know about Rachel?

He went over every detail he could remember since he'd taken the call. His only guess was that Natasha had overheard him, but he knew that didn't explain her comment. Rachel had done most of the talking, and the details Natasha had repeated to him had been thoughts he'd kept to himself.

He shouldn't jump to conclusions. Maybe Natasha had overheard another one of his phone calls with Rachel. She had said she wasn't used to running into people, so clearly this wasn't Natasha's first walk alone in the woods. If that wasn't weird enough, the older woman was as quiet as a doe as she moved along the forest path. But what he couldn't stop thinking about was the other thing she'd said.

If there were no secrets in a small town, did that mean Sarah knew about Rachel too? Will looked back towards the lodge, where the windows glowed yellow in the dim light of the late summer night. He felt like he'd finally found what he wanted in life, what he'd wanted for years. He hoped he wouldn't end up on the outside looking in.

* * *

"You're back just in time for dessert," Sarah said as Will walked in the door.

"Sorry I had to leave. Personal problem." He hoped that explanation would cut it, because he did not know how to explain further without giving everything away.

"Don't worry about it." Sarah's mom grinned. "We kept busy."

The wine bottle sat empty on the table, and Mac was pouring port for everyone. He shot Will a sideways glance. "You want some?"

Will wanted all the alcohol. He once again reminded himself that Natasha was no one to be afraid of. He was tempted to ask about her, but he didn't want Sarah or her family to think he was crazy. That seemed like a real possibility. Much more real than the chance that an old woman knew all the details of his personal life. "Yes, please."

Mac handed him a full glass, and Will thanked him with a nod. He tipped up the glass of sweet liquor. Could he still get that ride to the Buck? He looked at Sarah, but based on the amount of giggles coming from her, he had a feeling she was beyond driving.

Fine by him. He knew there was more booze in this house.

He sat down at the table and shoved a forkful of cherry pie and vanilla bean ice cream into his mouth while he listened to Sarah's family talk. Bart sensed Will's distress, and began to whine and try to sit by Will, no matter how many times he directed the dog back to his bed.

Mac excused himself first, claiming he had an early wake-up call for a flight. Sarah's mom asked him to help her back to the cabin, and Mac gladly obliged. Sarah's dad went with them, leaving just Will and Sarah, and half a bottle of port.

The thick drink soon made him feel more relaxed, and the syrupy sweet taste was addictive. He reached for the bottle to pour another glass, but accidentally knocked it over instead.

He jumped up from his chair. "Oh God, I am so sorry."

Will watched with horror as the spilled port turned the tablecloth from white to reddish purple.

"It's okay." Sarah swiftly moved everything off the table and gathered up the cloth. "I am going to get this in the washer."

She disappeared from the room, leaving Will and Bart on their own.

Will covered his eyes with his hands. It wasn't like him to be this clumsy. His head felt like sand, he was preoccupied, and if he was being honest with himself, a little drunk. The panic had sobered him up a bit, though.

He made his way to the laundry room to apologize to Sarah. "I'm so sorry, I'll buy you another one. I'll clean up the dishes. Whatever I can do to make it better, just tell me."

He'd once spilled coffee on his and Rachel's sofa, and Rachel had practically divorced him right then and there. It was one of the biggest fights they'd ever had, all over a stupid coffee stain. He'd do anything to avoid a similar situation with Sarah.

Sarah dabbed at the stain and loaded the tablecloth into the washer. "Don't worry about it. I can deal with a tablecloth."

He took a step towards her just as she turned to step back into the kitchen.

Then, before he could stop to think, Sarah was looking up

at him, and then her hands were on either side of his face. She pulled his mouth down to meet her own and brushed her lips over his.

Her kiss was even better than he remembered. Her touch set his body on fire, and suddenly Will couldn't get close enough. With a growl, he swooped her up, plunking her down on the dryer.

Sarah wrapped her legs around him, and he let out a moan as desire surged through him.

She pulled his shirt over his head and sucked in a breath as she ran her hands over his body. His heart slammed into his ribs as he watched her fingertips trail over his skin.

He kissed her again, the whirling sound of the washing machine muting her whimper. She was gorgeous. Sweet, and perfect, and gorgeous.

Sarah pulled away and licked her lips. "Your room?"

Will didn't have to be asked twice.

CHAPTER FIFTEEN

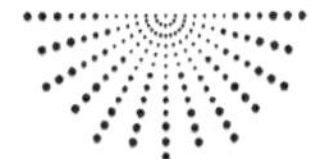

SARAH

Sarah's eyes flew open. Daylight filled the room as a man snored softly beside her.

She smiled to herself. So it hadn't been a dream.

Then her face warmed as she recalled the night before. After the laundry room, they'd made their way to Will's bedroom, where she'd broken her rule not to sleep with a man she worked with again, and again. Whatever Will's story was, this definitely wasn't his first time with a woman.

She gazed out the window at the evergreen trees and the bright gray sky, and for just a moment she could remember what life had been like back when she was young and in love —and unhurt.

Will moved beside her, wrapped his arms around her and pulled her close.

"Good morning, beautiful," he whispered into her ear.

Sarah squirmed, a delightful tingle traveling down her back. "Good morning."

She peeked at the digital clock on the nightstand, and let

out a sigh when she saw the date. Their first guests would arrive today. "I've got to get up."

Will opened one blue eye, squeezing it shut again when he saw the time. "No human has to get up right now," he grumbled as he kept her pinned to the bed beneath his muscled arm.

"This human does," she said with a poke to his shoulder. "I promise you'll get breakfast out of this."

His arm raised in an instant, and Sarah giggled. She gave him a soft kiss on the lips before she got up to collect her clothes.

When she was showered and dressed, she went to start the coffee pot. Bart followed her downstairs, his nails clicking against the wooden staircase. As the smell of a French roast filled the kitchen, Sarah whipped up a frittata and stuck it in the oven. They could eat the leftovers for lunch with a side salad. Her life of leisure was over—she would cook three full meals a day again, starting with dinner tonight. Will might be happy with scrambled eggs and turkey sandwiches day after day, but for the prices the guests paid, she knew they would not.

She went to set the timer on her watch, but she didn't have it on. She checked the living room, office, and bathroom before realizing where it had to be.

Sarah crept back into Will's room and grabbed her watch from the dresser. As she turned to leave, her eyes glimpsed something bright red outside. She moved closer to the window, and her eyebrows shot up. Sure enough, someone in a bright red rain jacket was walking around on their property. With the person's hood up, Sarah couldn't see much more than the skinny pair of blue jean legs below the jacket.

The lodge didn't have a fence, and property lines were pretty meaningless on the island. Everybody knew everybody, after all.

But Sarah had no idea who this was. Maybe a guest who'd arrived early? Or someone new in town?

Whoever it was, she intended to find out.

Sarah flew down the stairs and pulled on her rain boots as she went out the front door. She circled around to the side of the house where she'd seen Red Jacket. It only took half a second to spot the bright color in the dark forest.

"Hello," she called out. "Can I help you?"

Red Jacket turned around, and Sarah's face fell. "Mom?"

* * *

HER MOM'S SHOULDERS DROOPED. "Hi, honey. You're up early."

"It's the first day of check-ins." Plus, she'd spent the night in Will's room, so her whole routine was messed up. Not that her mom needed to know that. "You're up early too."

Her mom shuffled her feet. "You know I've always been an early riser. Even before I was older, I—"

Sarah held up her hand and tried to keep her voice from shaking. "What I meant to say is, you're up early and moving around well for someone who had a fall bad enough to incapacitate her and make her walk with a limp as recently as when she came over for dinner last night."

Her mom's face turned as red as her rain jacket. "Can we talk in the house?"

Sarah spun on her heel, and walked back to the lodge. Her mom followed her in silence.

Back in the kitchen, Sarah poured them both a cup of coffee. She took a deep breath and reminded herself not to yell. Will had hopefully been able to go back to sleep, and if he had, she didn't want to wake him up.

Her mom perched on a barstool on the other side of the kitchen island from Sarah.

Sarah pushed one of the mugs towards her mom. "Talk. I am trying not to jump to conclusions, but it's not easy."

Her mom looked at her hands. "I did fall, you see. I was hurt. Mac made a bigger deal about it than it was, of course."

Sarah nodded. She knew how her brother could be. He accused everyone else of being dramatic when he was the biggest drama queen in the northern hemisphere. "Of course he did."

Her mom took a sip of the coffee, her hand unsteady as she set the mug down. "So we didn't know how I would feel this summer, if maybe we should close the lodge. Then Mac had the idea that you could come and help. Your father and I didn't think it would work. We understand after everything that happened…"

Her voice trailed off, and she looked up at Sarah.

"I'm fine, Mom. Keep going."

"When you agreed to come back, your dad and I realized we hadn't had a vacation since, well, ever. We had so many things we wanted to do. Go to Italy. See giraffes. See turquoise waters for a change."

Sarah clenched her fists. It wasn't the first time she'd been lied to by someone she loved, but that didn't make it hurt any less. "So you thought what? Thought I would stay here indefinitely while you went to Europe, and Africa, and the Caribbean? I had a career, Mom. A life. I thought you loved me. Now I feel, I don't know. I feel tricked."

Her mom's eyes grew watery as she reached out towards Sarah. "Oh, honey. It was wrong, I know. I'm so sorry. I understand if you want to go back to California. We can take over. Will's such a big help, and your dad and I can do this with him. We'll buy your ticket back."

Sarah rubbed the back of her neck, deciding not to mention she knew her parents couldn't afford a one-way flight anywhere right now. "That's a nice idea, except I don't have a job anymore."

Her mom paled. "But it's not even been a full month, and you worked there for years, and…"

"I know." Sarah interrupted her. She had already tortured herself with the same thoughts. "But Los Angeles isn't a small town in Alaska, okay? You can't expect people to do you any favors."

Her mom's face crumpled up. "Oh God, I'm so sorry. I never dreamed that would happen."

Sarah wanted to be mad. She wanted to rage, and throw her coffee mug across the room, and pull her hair out. But she was starting to realize what her leaving Alaska had cost her parents.

Sarah had barely spoken to them in all her time away, and she'd never come back to visit. Her parents had offered to visit her in California, but Sarah had asked them not to. She hadn't wanted a single reminder of home. Sarah may have lost the love of her life that summer, but her parents had lost their only daughter.

With a sigh, Sarah walked around the kitchen island to wrap her mom in a hug. "It's okay. We'll figure it out."

Her mom let out a sob, and Sarah's heart squeezed. Why had she always assumed she was the only one who had been hurt five years ago?

Her mom stuck her head up and sniffed the air. "Is something burning?"

Sarah frowned. Then she remembered the frittata. "Shit!"

She ran to the oven, opening the door to a billow of smoke. "I hate this damn oven."

CHAPTER SIXTEEN

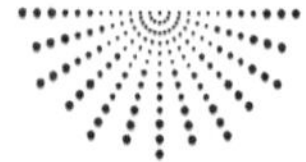

SARAH

If there was ever a good time for bad news, it was now. Even though Sarah was still processing the fact that her mom had lied to her, the lodge kept her too busy to think. All these years Sarah had been throwing herself into her work in LA when she could've been doing the same thing right here.

They had a full house almost right off the bat. It seemed that for every passenger Mac picked up for a return flight, he brought back two more. Sarah didn't stop moving from the minute she got up to the minute she went to bed. If she wasn't checking people in or answering questions, she was making food or cleaning rooms.

When the guests went to bed at night, she stayed up doing the bookkeeping on the new computer program she'd had Mac pick up in Juneau. Running the lodge was like riding a bike. A painful, emotional bike, but a bike all the same.

How different doing this had been as a kid, when she'd only helped her mom and dad. Now everything fell on her. Well, her and Will.

Sarah pinched the bridge of her nose. She had been up since four this morning, and it was almost midnight. But she had to get these reservations figured out. She rubbed her eyes but the gritty feeling didn't go away.

They needed a new system. The thick date book her parents had always used to keep track of reservations was too vulnerable to human error, and unfortunately, Sarah was far from perfect.

She made a note to ask Mac to pick up a software program in Juneau. Her shoulders tensed at the thought of yet another expense, but what could she do? She was over-whelmed by the amount of people wanting to book a stay at the lodge. How ironic was it that she, herself, couldn't wait to get out of here?

Not that she had much of a life to go back to.

A wave of nausea passed through her, and Sarah pushed her chair back so she could rest her head on her desk. Maybe if she closed her eyes for just a few minutes, she would feel better…

Sarah blinked her eyes open, her mind foggy. A hand rested on her shoulder. "Will?"

His smile sent a tingle down her back. "Hey, sleepy head. Why don't you go to bed?"

Sarah cleared her throat, opening up the reservation book to the page she had marked. She only had the brainpower to focus on one thing at a time. It didn't matter how cute Will was, work came first. "I'm not tired."

Will tapped his cheek. "You have a little something right here."

She wiped at her face where saliva had dribbled down from her mouth, and cringed. How attractive. "Thanks for waking me up. I still have a ton to do. Once I'm done here, I am going to prep lunch for tomorrow."

"Done," he said.

"What?"

"Sandwiches are made. Lunch bags are packed. Dishes are done…"

She frowned. "You didn't have to do that."

Will lifted his hands. "Hey, I'm not too worried about my job description."

Her eyes burned. Sarah didn't deserve someone like Will. But the truth was she'd be lost without him. "Thank you."

He settled into the chair across from her. "You see, I was hoping if I took all that off your plate, you would finally tell me what's wrong."

She pressed her lips together and looked away. Will had been pestering her since the morning she'd run into her mom, but she didn't want to tell him. The last thing she needed was for him to know what a loser she was.

"Sarah, please look at me," he said softly.

She looked up, and his blue gaze held hers. Sometimes it was like he could see right through her. "It's nothing, Will."

He reached out, taking her hand and giving it a squeeze. "It's not nothing. And it's clearly bothering you. Please talk to me."

Her throat tightened up. No, she didn't deserve Will at all.

Sarah took a deep breath. The truth was, Will had not once let her down. He did his job, helped her with hers, and had even pulled her out of the water that day on the dock. The least she could do was tell him what had happened. "That morning after we were together…"

His eyes darkened, and Sarah felt her cheeks flush. She still couldn't go into the damn laundry room without thinking of him. "I remember."

Sarah looked away, breaking his gaze. "I ran into my mom. She's fine, Will. She fell, but she wasn't hurt. Not as bad as they led me to believe. They all lied to me to get me back to Alaska."

Will was by her side in an instant. He knelt down and looked her in the eye. "Oh, Sarah. Why didn't you just tell me?"

Her eyes burned at the pity in his voice. "Because I felt like an idiot. Because I'm used to dealing with everything alone."

"But you're not alone. I'm here."

Sarah swallowed. She had forgotten how wonderful it was to care about someone. To be cared about. "You're too damn easy to like, do you know that?"

He lifted one corner of his mouth. "So it's working."

"What's working?"

He waggled his eyebrows. "My plan to get you into bed."

A wave of desire crashed through her body. Only Will could turn her mood around in ten seconds flat. Sarah shook her head, trying to clear her mind. She turned back to her desk and picked up the date book. "Not right now. I've got a million more things to do. And I'm exhausted."

"That's why I suggested it." Will took the date book from her hand and pulled her to her feet. He wrapped one arm around her back and looped the other under her legs, picking her up. "You're going to bed. And you're going to sleep in. No alarm. That's an order."

She frowned as she looped her arms around his neck. "But what about breakfast? And checkouts? And the rooms?"

Will pressed a kiss to her temple, turning her stomach to mush. "Those are my problems. Your job is to sleep. I don't know how to fix everything for you, no matter how much I'd like to. But I can at least make sure you get some rest."

Sarah wanted to insist she could handle it. She wasn't expecting Will to save her all the time. She couldn't. But something about the rhythm of his steps as he carried her, and the way Bart pranced behind, and Will's minty smell where her face was pressed into his chest made all her resolutions fade away.

Was it so wrong to let someone take care of her? Was it so wrong to enjoy it?

She closed her eyes and snuggled her head under Will's chin, the scruff there scratchy against her forehead. "Are you sure you can't join me? Everyone's asleep. If you keep working, you'll just wake them up."

He grunted as he climbed the stairs. "Then we really are in a predicament. Because if I come to bed with you, we'll definitely wake them up."

Her face warmed. "I think it'll be okay."

Will shifted her in his arms as he reached to open the door to her room. He set her on her feet, pinning her with his gaze. "Oh you do, do you?"

Sarah bit her lip and nodded.

Will leaned forward and covered her mouth with his. She melted into the kiss, every worry from the day fading away. All that mattered was this moment, this man.

Maybe she didn't deserve Will. But that didn't mean she didn't want him.

CHAPTER SEVENTEEN

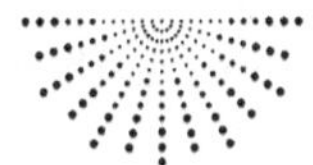

WILL

Bart rested his head on his paws with a sigh, his beady eyes locked in on Will.

Will ran a hand through his hair. "I know. I'm an idiot."

His grand declarations from the beginning of summer had faded away, replaced with thoughts of Sarah. So much for not getting involved.

He reached into the laundry basket, grabbed the clean fitted sheet, and stretched it over the bed with a grunt. Just as he was about to loop it around the last corner, it snapped back and collapsed in a shriveled heap on the mattress.

Will let out a curse word and started over. How the hell did single people do it? He looked at Bart. "You could help, you know."

Bart whined and looked away.

Luckily, this was the last bedroom to clean today.

When Will had volunteered to handle the housekeeping while Sarah took care of things in the kitchen, she'd looked at him as if he was superman. Which was laughable. Will felt old. He was divorced, or at least about to be, and the business he'd spent years building was gone. If wanting to make Sarah happy made him superman in her eyes, he'd take it.

He finished making the bed, smoothing out the quilt. Then he piled the dirty sheets in the laundry basket and snapped his fingers. "Let's go."

Bart pranced behind him as they made their way to the laundry room, where Will loaded the dirty sheets, and started the washer.

He shivered. He couldn't hear the damn thing get started without thinking of Sarah and that first, well second, kiss.

Actually, it'd be harder to find something that didn't make him think of Sarah. For a man who'd started the summer swearing off women, he was doing a poor job of it. But it had been an impossible resolution to stick to when the most amazing woman he had ever met had become his roommate.

When he'd sat in the attorney's office across from Rachel, he'd wished for a hole to open in the ground and swallow him up. Now he felt like he should write his ex-wife a thank you note. After years of just existing, Will finally remembered what it felt like to feel alive. He remembered what it was like to be in love.

He found Sarah in the kitchen scrubbing the serving trays from breakfast. Her face was twisted in concentration, her hair was escaping from her ponytail in wisps that pointed every which way, and her shirt was splashed with dish water.

A wave of desire passed through him—she'd never looked more beautiful.

He wrapped his arms around her and pressed a kiss to her neck. She wiggled against him, and heat shot through his body.

"When's break time?" he murmured in her ear.

She swatted at him with a soapy hand. "We have guests, you know."

"You're no fun." He stepped back to lean against the kitchen island. "Okay, captain. I finished the rooms. What's next?"

Sarah sighed. "I've got paperwork to do, but you should take a break."

"But I want to help."

She turned off the water, wiping her hands on a dish towel. "You're doing too much, Will. Seriously. Take a break."

He smiled. He didn't need a break. Helping Sarah, making her happy, filled his body with the kind of buzzing energy a person couldn't even get from sleep. "I'll take a break when you do."

Sarah laughed. "Then you're going to be waiting a long time. I worked here every single summer growing up, and I don't remember a single break. I didn't even leave to go to college. I couldn't. My parents wouldn't have been able to run this place by themselves."

He folded his arms over his chest. Did the incessant work pace have something to do with why Sarah had left Alaska before? "But you're doing it by yourself now."

She sighed. "Not really. You're here. And even then, it's not easy."

He watched her face closely. "Does it bother you? That you never got to go to college?"

Sarah shook her head. "No. My parents did their best."

"What about your brother? Did he go to school?"

She snorted. "Mac? No way. He loves it here."

Will chuckled. "That's ironic, since he seems to hate everything else."

Sarah quirked up one side of her mouth. "I know he's rough around the edges, but he means well."

"Maybe he's protective of you."

She set her hand on her chest. "Of me? You remember that he's the one who came to California, lied to my face and dragged me back to Alaska, right? If Mac's protective of anything, it's his own way of life. He's single for a reason."

Will smirked. "Oh, so that's the problem. He's jealous that you have a life and he doesn't."

Sarah barked a laugh "I have a life? Have you looked around lately? I'm unemployed and stuck in Alaska."

He took a step towards her, the words tumbling out of his mouth before he could stop them. "You do have something going for you. I happen to know of an average looking handyman who has a crush on you."

She blushed. "A crush, huh?"

He smiled, brushing a stray hair from her face. "Can you blame me? You make, like, really good scrambled eggs."

She laughed, and her cheeks turned rosy. "You know I can't cook."

Will hooked his fingers through the belt loops of her jeans and pulled her closer. "Then you're doing one hell of a job pretending. You have me fooled."

Sarah snuggled into his chest, and Will's heart squeezed. God, he could stay like this forever.

"I don't deserve you." She sighed, and he could feel her warm breath through the thin fabric of his t-shirt. His heart stretched in his chest.

Will stepped back, placed his hands on her shoulders, and looked her in the eye. "I'm the lucky one here."

She opened her mouth as if to say something, but closed it again. With a small smile, she reached up to give him a kiss. "For the record, I think this qualifies as a break. Now I have a stack of paperwork waiting for me."

Will laughed as he watched her walk away—he'd never

met anyone like her. He'd meant what he said. He was the lucky one.

He knew Sarah didn't like being back in Alaska, but to Will, this place was magical. To the point where he was starting to believe he could have everything he wanted.

CHAPTER EIGHTEEN

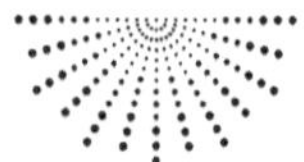

SARAH

Sarah hit save on the accounting program and slumped in the chair. Her back ached after being hunched over the keyboard for hours, but she had finally caught up. At least for today.

A glance at her watch told her she'd have to start dinner soon.

She patted her lap, and Bart jumped up. Her shoulders relaxed as she scratched the small dog's ears and he rolled his head appreciatively around in her hand.

A light knock came at the door, and Sarah quickly corrected her frown into a smile. She always told guests if they couldn't find her, they should check her office. "Come in."

The door swung open, and Sarah let out a sigh of relief when she saw Will. "Everything okay?"

Will nodded, stepping inside the office to close the door behind him. He eyed Bart, who was practically asleep in Sarah's lap, and shook his head. "Traitor."

He turned his attention to Sarah. "I am going to handle things at the lodge tonight."

She frowned. "What? Why?"

"Because you have dinner plans. Your parents invited you over."

Sarah tensed up, and Bart shifted in her lap. "Not happening. You remember the part where my mom lied to me, and that I can't get my job back, right?"

Will folded his arms. "You remember the part where your parents aren't going to live forever and haven't been able to have you over for dinner in the past five years, right?"

She narrowed her eyes. "Why are you on their side all of a sudden?"

Will let out a sigh and shifted his feet. "Your dad said if you couldn't come over, then they would come here. He said it can't wait."

She rested her head back against the chair. Her parents knew Sarah wouldn't want a scene. She would go to their place to avoid any awkward conversations in front of guests. "Are you sure you can't go in my place?"

Will's face pinched together. "Negative. Mac is going to be there."

Sarah gave him a look. "You see the guy twice a day. And he's not that bad."

"To be accurate, I avoid him twice a day. Maybe he's nice to you, but it's pretty obvious he wouldn't lose any sleep if I weren't here." Will ran his hand through his hair. "How about I have a cold beer waiting for you here?"

"Two cold beers," Sarah countered.

"You have yourself a deal."

She sighed. "Fine. I guess I'll go."

Will stuck his lip out in a mock pout. "Fine? No thank you for me? I am covering the lodge after all. I have to make dinner."

Sarah laughed and shook her head. "You'll be okay. I have everything prepped for dinner, including a build-your-own-sundae bar, in the fridge. Homemade fudge sauce, the works. You can grill a burger, right?"

He grinned. "It's pretty much the only thing I can do."

Sarah's stomach did a flip flop—she knew for a fact there was a lot more he could do. Like kiss her until she lost track of which way was up.

Will opened the door and looked back at Bart. "Are you staying or going?"

The dog gave him a brief glance before lowering his head again.

Will rolled his eyes and headed back out.

Sarah watched the door close behind him. Not even the warmth of Bart's small body could chase off the chill that ran down her back.

Soon enough, Will would leave, and she would do this alone.

Maybe she could rest her eyes for two minutes before going back to work? But when her cell phone rang she was wide awake. In California, she'd been used to getting a million calls a day on her phone. These days the only calls she got were on the landline for the lodge. It seemed the outside world had all but forgotten her.

Aaron's name flashed across the screen, and Sarah raised an eyebrow.

They'd barely spoken since she came to Alaska. Once in a while, he would text her. Sarah had thought he was just being polite, although she didn't know why. Any chance of a second date was indefinitely on hold. "Hi Aaron. What's going on?"

"I'm not allowed to just call you and say hi?" he teased. "I hadn't heard from you in a while, that's all."

"Sorry," Sarah said. "It's been busy here."

He laughed. "I understand being busy."

Sarah cringed. Aaron likely understood better than her—he ran a huge tech company. Next to that, the lodge seemed like small potatoes.

"So, when are you coming back?"

She bit her lip. That was the million dollar question. "I wish I knew."

"Really? I'm kind of surprised. I know Desirae, and she's not exactly easy going."

Sarah gulped. There was no point in lying to him. It would seem less pathetic if she told him, rather than him finding out second hand. "That may be relevant if I still worked for her."

"What?"

She took a deep breath. "Yeah, my first month up here, she let me go."

"Why didn't you tell me?"

Sarah rubbed the back of her neck. She could hear the concern in his voice. But instead of comforting her, it made her feel guilty. Things weren't going anywhere with Aaron. He was wasting his time. "Would it have mattered? I had to stay here regardless."

"I'm sorry," Aaron said. "This is off the record, but Desirae's an idiot. You were the best I worked with."

"You're biased," she said.

"Can you blame me?" He asked, his voice husky.

At one time, his words would've set Sarah's body on fire. But that had been before she'd met Will. Now there was only one man she could think about.

Sarah shifted in her seat. "I'm sure you have more than work keeping you busy in Los Angeles."

"If that's the case, why do you think I'm still calling you?"

"I was wondering the same thing. I'm thousands of miles

away, and it's probably going to stay that way unless Desirae has a change of heart."

"You don't need Desirae," he said.

The hair on the back of her neck stood up. Where was this going? "Why's that?"

"I know someone who manages a pretty successful business. I think the HR department is hiring."

Sarah sat up in the chair, making Bart snort as he readjusted himself. "Aaron, you can't be serious. I don't need a pity job."

"It's not a pity job," he reassured her. "Maybe I just want you close by."

Sarah's mind raced. She didn't want to lead Aaron on. "I'm sorry, I—"

"Just think about it," he insisted.

"I will."

They ended the call, and Sarah stared at the phone on her desk. She didn't feel good about leading Aaron on. But the possibility of an out, of a way back to Los Angeles, was too good to pass up. At least for now.

Sarah's head throbbed. She just had to get through this dinner with her parents, through this summer, and then maybe she could move on with her life. She couldn't stay here with Will forever, Not that she wanted that. Or did she?

CHAPTER NINETEEN

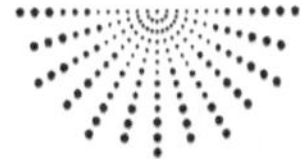

SARAH

Under normal circumstances, the trail back from her parent's cabin was a relaxing walk. The easy, flat path was protected from the rain by tall, bushy trees, giving it a cozy feel.

If only Sarah didn't have a rock in her stomach.

This wasn't happening. It wasn't possible. When her parents had invited her over for dinner, she had thought it was an excuse to apologize for turning her life upside down.

But there had been no apology, just her mom's big smile as she dropped the news.

"We've decided to sign the lodge over to you and Mac." She looked between them, her eyes sparkling. "It just makes sense, Sarah. You don't have a job anymore, and Mac loves it here."

Her parents seemed to think they were doing her some big favor, but they didn't know what she had gone through. She had never told anyone the full truth. That she was the reason Andre had left that day—she was the reason he was dead.

And now she was getting the punishment she deserved. The reality pressed down on her, surrounding her like the darkness of the night.

She was stuck here.

"You gonna pout the whole way home?"

Sarah's face heated. If she was upset with her parents, she was furious with Mac. He'd gone to California and lied to her face.

She stopped walking and turned to him. She knew that if she could get inside his head, she'd find a world where Mac did no wrong. "And just what the hell is your problem with me? It wasn't enough to drag me back to Alaska? You're still pissed I hired Will…"

Mac rolled his eyes. "I could've swung a hammer. Or you could've for that matter."

"With what time? You're always circling the air, and I'm busy cleaning rooms and balancing the books," Sarah snapped.

Her brother narrowed his eyes. "Don't make this about something it's not. I know you're falling for that guy. He's a total city slicker. And did you forget he's going to be gone at the end of summer? Oh wait, I forgot. That's your type."

Sarah gritted her teeth. "What is that supposed to mean?"

Mac snorted. "It means you don't want any real responsibility."

Her entire body felt hot as a wave of anger crashed over her. "Real responsibility? And what have you ever done? Sat your happy ass on this island for over thirty years, never moving even an hour away from your parents, and—"

"Enough," Mac growled. He glanced back towards the cabin. "They're going to hear you."

Sarah pushed past him. "I don't care. I need to go back there."

Mac clamped a hand on her arm. "Oh no, you don't."

She turned to glare at her brother. "You might be okay with this, but I am not. I have a life and dreams and none of them include waking up in my personal nightmare every day until I die."

Mac let go of her arm with a sigh. "Why didn't you tell me you lost your job?"

She stuck out her chin. "Why would I tell you? You'd just give me some speech about the fact that it was a crappy job, or that California is stupid. or how I should be thankful to be here. Whatever you'd say, it wouldn't make me feel better."

"You really think that?"

Sarah folded her arms. "I know that. You're only happy when I'm not. I don't know what I did to piss you off, but I'm not hanging around here. You can't watch me forever. I'm telling Mom and Dad the first chance I get."

They stood nose-to-nose, staring at each other. Though Sarah sometimes questioned if they were related, no one else ever would. Not with their matching green eyes, auburn hair, and dusting of freckles.

Mac broke the silence first, pulling his hand down his face. "I need a drink."

Sarah's mouth twitched. Mac had a lot of issues, but speaking his mind wasn't one of them. "And you think a drink is going to fix this?"

He shoved his hands into the pockets of his heavy canvas jacket. "Don't be ridiculous. I want to start with a drink here, and then I want to go to Wolfie's. That's where I do my good thinking."

Sarah knew there was no stopping him. She might as well ask the gray Alaskan sky to stop raining for all the good it would do. "Let's go then."

They walked the last few minutes to the lodge in silence, tiptoeing into the kitchen.

Sarah grabbed two beers, handing one to Mac.

He held up the bottle between his thumb and forefinger as if he wasn't sure what to do with it. "I need something stronger."

Sarah perched on a counter stool. "Save yourself for Wolfie's schnapps, then. Not even top shelf whiskey can come close to that."

Mac grunted and popped the cap off. He took a sip and looked at Sarah. "For the record, I'm not only happy when you suffer, okay? When you left, it left a big hole in my life. In all our lives."

Sarah swallowed, but the lump in her throat refused to move. She knew what Mac meant, because Andre had left a hole in her heart when he'd disappeared. It had almost broken her, and Sarah never wanted to go through that again.

But what about when Will wasn't here anymore? So far, he didn't have any plans past the end of the summer. At least nothing that he'd shared with Sarah. Still, she knew that one day he would be gone, and Sarah would once again be left behind to pick up the pieces.

She shivered. Mac had said it himself—that was her type.

Taking a sip of her beer, she tried to lighten the mood. "Are you sure you haven't been drinking already?"

Mac shook his head. "You're right. It's too early for that kind of talk."

Sarah picked at the label on her beer bottle, tiny shreds of paper piling up next to the amber glass.

"They say if you peel the label like that, it means you're sexually frustrated."

She stuck her tongue out at her brother. "No commentary on my romantic life, thank you very much."

Mac shuddered. "Fine by me. I sure as hell don't want to hear about you getting cozy with that beanpole who lives here."

He knew as well as Sarah that Will wasn't exactly a beanpole anymore. Non-stop physical labor and three square meals a day had seen to that. Her face warmed at the memory of Will's body next to hers. "If that were true, your label would be history."

Mac pulled up the rectangular sticker, tore it clean off, and let it curl in on itself.

Sarah burst into laughter. She couldn't help it, and after a moment, Mac let out a rare chuckle, too.

Mac tossed the trash on the counter. "Not exactly a great dating scene on the island."

Sarah took a pull of her beer. "Then why do you stay?"

Her brother lifted a shoulder. "There's nowhere else I want to go."

"Mom and Dad should give this all to you. That would make more sense."

He peered at her. "You trying to escape again?"

Sarah felt her body grow tense. Why couldn't things ever be easy with Mac? "I'm trying to be nice, okay? I know you don't believe this, but I am not actually always thinking of myself."

"Sorry," he muttered. "I don't know. I'll think about it. Sure as heck ain't going anywhere."

"But you're lonely. Don't you want to meet someone?"

Mac gestured to the lodge. "Look around. What woman would be okay with this? How many people have left over the years? I doubt I could bring anyone here and convince her to stay, and it's slim pickings in town. No thanks. I know what I want—I've accepted that no one else wants the same thing."

A small, fine line cracked in Sarah's heart. Mac was

lonely, and he was going to make sure he stayed that way. Was she doing the same thing?

"Just think about it," she said. "Now, are we going to get this party started, or what?"

CHAPTER TWENTY

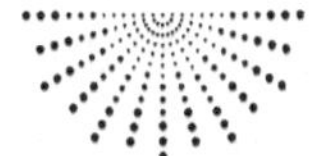

WILL

Something pressed against Will's shoulder. He blinked his eyes open to see the outline of a heart-shaped face, hair falling around it like a halo.

Was he dreaming? He cleared his throat. "Sarah?"

He'd gone to bed after making sure he'd taken care of all the tasks Sarah would have needed to do. The dinner dishes had been washed and put away, all the guests were confirmed back from their adventures around the island, and bacon was thawing for tomorrow's breakfast.

He'd wondered how it had all gone with her parents, but he hadn't wanted it to seem like he was sitting up and waiting for her. As if she wasn't an adult who had made it thirty years in life without him.

Now Sarah smiled at him, her teeth reflecting white in the light that came from the hallway. "It's me."

Will sat up on his elbows. Sarah had only come to his room once before, and even thinking about that night made his body respond. "Is everything okay?"

"We're going to the Buck. Mac invited you to come with us. Want to come?"

Will frowned. "Is he drunk?"

Sarah giggled. "He plans to be."

Will had a feeling they had both been drinking, which made him wonder what the heck had happened at dinner. Were they celebrating? Or drowning their sorrows? "Okay, I'll come. But one condition. I'm driving."

She gave a careful wink. "You got it."

Oh yeah. He was driving.

Will shooed Sarah from his room so he could change into jeans.

"Why?" She snickered as she left. "I've seen it all before."

Sarah and Mac were waiting for him when he made it downstairs.

Will ran a hand through his hair. "What about the guests?"

"That's why we gotta be quiet, city slicker," Mac whispered.

He and Sarah tiptoed past Will, though neither of them were very quiet, fighting back giggles.

With a shake of his head, Will grabbed the keys to the truck, and they all piled into the cab.

Will and Sarah had only gone together to the Buck that one time. If Will was being honest, which there was no point not to be in the small town, he had stopped in for a beer and a quick bite a few times when picking up orders from the store. But he had never been to the Buck on a Friday night, and nothing could've prepared him for it.

Somehow, the tiny population on the island had filled the building, making it feel more like a busy nightclub in Seattle than a small town watering hole. Rock music blared, beer flowed, and Will wondered if he was still in Darling. But then again, he guessed there was nowhere else in town for people to go.

Wolfie greeted them with a grin as they made their way through the crowd.

"Three beers," Mac said. "And three schnapps."

Will waited for Mac to turn away, before leaning towards Wolfie. Will had learned his lesson with schnapps before, and he wanted to be sure he could drive them all home safely. "None for me."

Wolfie acknowledged him with a nod, deftly filling a third shot glass with water.

Once the three of them slammed the empty glasses on the bar top, they turned to find a booth. Will sat between Sarah and one of the fishermen he'd crossed paths with at the store a time or two. Community seating clearly wasn't a new concept around here.

Will was thankful he'd taken the keys. His suspicion that the two Carter siblings had been drinking before they'd invited him to take part in their night was soon confirmed. Their smiles were too easy for just one shot. Sarah was small, but there was no way the shot of liquor they'd had at the bar had affected someone of Mac's size that much.

Will's phone buzzed in his pocket, and he wrinkled his forehead. He didn't need a clock to know it was late. That the summer sky had finally gotten dark told him that.

Will looked at his phone. Another text from Rachel asking how he was doing. She'd been checking in more and more often as the countdown clock to when their divorce would be finalized continued to tick. She'd ask about Bart or some-times questions about the business. She seemed to talk to him more now than she had when they'd been together. Will wondered how things were between her and Jason. They had what they wanted. Their relationship wasn't a secret, they had the company, and Rachel had unchecked access to all the money that came with it. He hoped they hadn't run it into the ground yet, but then that would have been a record even for his shopaholic wife. Soon to be shopaholic ex-wife.

He shoved the phone back into his pocket. He wasn't in the mood to chat, and the last thing he needed was for Rachel to get the idea that Will was available to her at all hours of the day.

Sarah leaned in. "You okay?"

He caught a faint scent of liquor on her breath. For some stupid reason, having her close like this, gave him the warm fuzzies. He smiled. "Just fine."

"I think you need another drink."

He held up his beer, still mostly full. "I'm good."

She glanced around the room. "A dance then?"

A few tables had been cleared out in the middle of the room to make space for the men and women who twirled around in rhythm to the music. It wasn't so much dancing as movement, but again, the competition for entertainment around here was slim.

With a smile, he offered his arm to Sarah. "Yes to the dance."

He felt the looks they got as they walked to the makeshift dance floor as clearly as if he were being tapped on the shoulder. He would bet money that he and Sarah would be the main topic of the gossip mill tomorrow morning. But Will had never been one to care about what other people thought.

A fast-paced song came on, and they hopped around the floor with everyone else as the crowd sang along with the lyrics. It was a classic, if a few decades old. His clothes grew damp with sweat as they moved across the dance floor, and he laughed. He couldn't remember the last time he'd had this much fun. Heck, he couldn't remember having fun, period.

After a few more songs, a slow one came on. Will shot a sharp look toward Wolfie, who merely shrugged as he walked away from the jukebox. Couples paired off, and Will and Sarah moved closer together. Something about her warm body and the late night, the energy of the music, and the crowded bar made everything feel alright. As they swayed, Will wished the song would never end, wished the summer would never end.

But this was Alaska, and the summer was as short as love stories. He barely knew Sarah, and he wasn't yet divorced. This place wasn't his life. And if he was being honest with himself, he needed to figure his life out from scratch, as a single man without his own business. But knowing all that changed nothing; he wanted to stay right here.

Sarah leaned her head into him, and Will's heart moved in his chest. This wasn't love, he told himself again.

But it was something.

The song ended, and Sarah looked up at him, blinking slowly.

She stepped away. "I'll be right back."

Will headed back to the table where Sarah's purse and both their jackets sat, untouched. Darling was the only place on earth where that fact didn't surprise Will.

The table wiggled as Mac sat down holding two beers, the foam sliding down the glass.

Will held up a hand. "Thanks, but I have a drink already."

Mac hiccuped. "I drank it."

Will furrowed his brow. "You drank my beer?"

"Yep. It was going warm while you were out there getting cozy with my sister. Which, by the way, you pretty much have to marry her now. The whole town is here tonight, and you have no secrets anymore."

"So that's the rule? If you dance with someone, you have to get married? Tough to be new in town."

Mac snorted into his beer. "Don't be ridiculous. It's not true for everyone. Just people who make lovey dovey eyes at each other and dance real close. I know you two aren't just coworkers."

"You'll be relieved to know I won't be your brother-in-law. I'm not going to marry your sister just because we danced in public."

He decided it wasn't worth mentioning that he was technically still married already, though he'd be officially divorced in just over a month.

Mac downed half of his pint. "Suit yourself. You could do worse than Sarah. Where is she, by the way?"

Will searched the crowd, but he didn't see her auburn head anywhere. He stood up to get a better view. "Not sure. I'll take a look around."

Will left Mac behind and wove through the crowd where more than one familiar face gave him a smile. When he still didn't find Sarah, he went to the back and waited outside the women's restroom. It was the last place he could think of. When the door finally opened, Wolfie's wife stepped out, making the both of them jump. Will had barely spoken to her during his previous visits to the Buck, though she'd always been nice, if shy.

Will gave her an apologetic smile. "Sorry. I wasn't trying to be a creep. I was looking for Sarah."

"It's okay, honey, I saw her go out back."

Will headed in the direction she pointed. It was news to him that there was a back area to the Buck, but when he stepped out of a creaky door, he found a couple of wood benches and several plastic lawn chairs. Smokers talked loudly where they sat in a circle, with drinks in their free hands.

At last he saw Sarah sitting alone on a bench, her shoulders hunched.

"Hey," he said softly as he approached her. "You okay?"

She gave a single nod, a cigarette dangling from her hand. She held it to her mouth, and a red glow shone in the night.

Will had never tried a cigarette in his life. He couldn't even stand cigars, and he knew those were supposed to be classy. "I didn't know you smoked."

She exhaled. "I don't. Unless I'm pretty drunk, like right now."

"Can I join you?"

She patted the spot next to her.

Will settled in, careful to keep space between her shoulder and his. Otherwise, they would probably have to get married *and* have kids. "Do you want to go home?"

When she didn't answer, he looked at her face to see a glistening trail from her eyes to her chin.

His stomach sank. "Oh God, I'm so sorry. I didn't know you were crying. Is it something I did?"

She sniffed and wiped her nose on the back of her hand. "It's just that, it's exactly that. You're too damn nice. Too easy to like."

"What do you mean?"

"I mean, I never wanted to come back here. I never wanted to fall in love again. And here I am, doing both."

His heart raced. "You're falling in love?"

Sarah took another inhale of the cigarette. "Yes. Maybe. I don't know."

Her voice was ragged, raw, like she'd been upset for a while and held it back while it had been wearing at her from the inside.

"Sarah, I'm not going anywhere."

"Not until your contract is up," she reminded him.

"But what if I stayed?"

She turned to look at him, her eyes two giant pools.

"Don't you see that's part of the problem? I shouldn't want you to stay. But for some stupid reason, I do."

She let out a heavy sigh. "I don't know what I want anymore. I don't trust myself, and neither should you."

The words welled up in his chest. He needed to tell her. Tell her he couldn't promise anything except to see where this went, that he had been married but not in love, not like what they had. That he'd stay for her, that he would stay for as long as they both wanted it.

Any of those things would have been better than saying nothing, better than leaving her adrift in her pain and loneliness.

But he never got the chance. Sarah jumped up from the bench and ran behind the building to where the first few lonely trees stood before they gathered into a thick forest.

Will followed her in time to hear retching. He could only see the outline of her body, doubled over with one hand resting against a birch tree.

He'd never considered himself to have a strong stomach, but that didn't stop him from walking up to her and softly patting her back.

When she'd finished emptying her stomach, he told her it was time to go home.

CHAPTER TWENTY-ONE

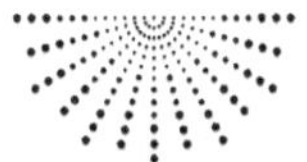

Sarah didn't remember much from that night at the Buck, but what she could remember, she didn't want to.

She had poured her heart out to Will, and he hadn't said a word.

Sarah had long suspected she was an idiot when it came to love. Now she knew it to be a fact.

Like a true idiot, she'd held her breath, waiting for him to say something. Anything. Some acknowledgement that he cared about her feelings, even if he didn't return them. A week had gone by, and he hadn't said a thing. As the time passed, Sarah only felt worse.

When Aaron's name popped up on her phone, she was surprised. Last time they'd talked, Sarah had promised she'd think about the job, but there had really been nothing to think about. Aaron had only offered her the job out of pity, and he'd forget about her soon enough.

She waited until late morning, when most of the guests had left for the day, breakfast had been cleaned up, and Will was working outside. Then she holed up in the office and locked the door behind her to guarantee privacy before she opened up her laptop.

Music trilled, and she clicked to connect the video chat with Aaron.

He greeted her with a grin, looking better on video than most people did in real life. The last time she'd seen him, he'd been leaning back on white bed sheets. Sarah didn't regret her time with Aaron. He'd always been a gentleman, and he'd treated her well.

She waited for her stomach to do flip-flops at the memories, but it sat heavy with this morning's breakfast. Something had to be wrong with her. Why couldn't she just be normal and like the sexy millionaire back?

"So, are you really in Alaska, or is that just a cover story? Did you take a job with someone else?"

Sarah laughed. "I hate to disappoint you, but yes, I really am in Alaska."

Aaron let out a whistle. "Honestly, it's a bit of a relief. Otherwise, it would make it a lot harder to convince you."

"Convince me of what?"

"To take that job offer I told you about, working with me."

Sarah shifted in her seat. Aaron was a millionaire. Correction. He was a multi-millionaire. A handsome, funny, charming, multi-millionaire. He should date an actress or an heiress, so why was he still talking to her? "I am flattered, but—"

"Just let me talk. You were one of the best I ever worked with. Professional. Dependable. Tireless."

He named her job duties, benefits, and a salary that nearly made her eyes roll out of her head. "I am going to email you the contract. Just think about it."

Sarah swallowed. It had to be said. "You remember my, um, policy, right?"

"It's burned into my brain. But I found the loophole."

She cocked her head to the side. "Loophole?"

"I would be the boss this time." He winked. "Let me know."

Aaron disappeared from the screen, and Sarah refreshed her email until the contract came through moments later.

She chewed her lip raw, reading every word. If ever in her life something had been too good to be true, this was it.

She didn't know what to think. However, she very much wanted to know what one person thought of all this.

* * *

WILL TURNED over the last page. "This is impressive. It's a substantial offer. But I'd still have your attorney look it over."

Sarah accepted the stack of papers back from him. "Right. My attorney."

He peered at her. "You have an attorney, right?"

She swallowed. "Should I? I've never needed one. Or I thought I didn't."

"You're going to want to find one now. I doubt there is someone in Darling. Mine is in Seattle, so that's no help. Who did your parents use for the deed to the lodge?"

"I'll have to ask them." She twirled a lock of hair around her finger. "What have you used an attorney for? Did something happen?"

Will seemed to pale slightly. "I have one just in case."

She nodded. There had to be more to the story, but if Will didn't want to tell her the details, she would not push. "So you think I should take the offer? After I get someone to look it over, of course."

Will cleared his throat. "I can tell you it's an excellent offer. You're the only one who knows if you should take it or not. Of course, you'd have to leave Alaska again. But you said your place in California is still available."

Sarah glanced down at the contract again. The lease was coming up in two months. She had thought she would have to let it go, but maybe this job would change everything. "The salary would probably be of more help to my parents than me working at the lodge. Mac could hire someone, and I could pitch in."

"So you're going to go work in California and send money back home to keep this place running? Why not just sell?"

She looked up at him. "I can't. It's my parent's dream. And all Mac wants is to be here."

Will held her gaze, his blue eyes seeing things she didn't want him to. "What's your dream?"

Her mouth went dry. Her dream was to go back in time. Not send Andre away. Not have kept the guilt, anger, and loneliness alive for the past five years. Her dream was to feel normal. "I don't know."

"Think about it before you sign that offer. You gotta do something, right? It won't be summer forever."

He was right. According to the calendar, it was still summer. But the weather had turned. Already the days had grown shorter, colder. Soon it would be mostly dark and the rain even heavier.

"What about you? What's your plan?"

He ran a hand through his hair. "I guess I have to think about that, too."

"You still don't have another job lined up?"

"Not yet."

Sarah bit the inside of her cheek. She had never met someone so relaxed about money. Will acted like those trust fund kids she'd met in Los Angeles, the ones who knew that when they swiped their cards, the money would be there.

Their attitude had made sense, but she hadn't expected the same one from a handyman. "Think you'll stay in Alaska?"

"Will you?" he asked.

Her heart sunk a little deeper. If he needed her to say it first, he would have to wait a lifetime. She'd tried that night at the Buck, and he'd given her nothing in return. Even now, when he had the perfect opportunity, when she was asking him what they should do, he held his cards close to his chest.

More proof she was stupid. Aaron was offering her the world on a silver platter, and she was too busy wondering what some man who couldn't care less thought about her.

She hopped off the counter stool. "Thanks for taking the time to look at this."

"Sarah, wait!" Will called after her.

Her heart slammed into her chest as she turned to face him. This was it. This was her fairytale moment. Just like in the movies, right when the heroine had given up hope, this was the light in the storm.

"Make sure you run that by an attorney before you agree to anything."

Her throat tightened. "I will."

She didn't know if taking this job was the right thing. She didn't know what she wanted to do. But she knew without a shadow of a doubt that Will Brooks did not care about her.

CHAPTER TWENTY-TWO

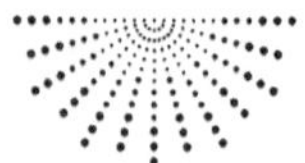

WILL

Bart licked Will's face again. Even his dog was feeling bad for him. Will let out a moan and pulled the covers back over his head. He knew he had to get up, but his head felt thick with exhaustion after tossing and turning all night.

In his marriage, they'd both been at fault. Rachel had done her fair share of damage, like cheating with his best friend. But Will knew he wasn't innocent in the breakdown of their relationship, either. He had worked tirelessly, always chasing the next milestone. He'd thought at the time that he'd been doing the right thing by providing a lifestyle neither of them could have had imagined before. But now he wondered if that wasn't where the problems had truly begun. He hadn't been available to Rachel, so she'd found someone who was.

And now he had messed up with Sarah. He hadn't been able to stop thinking about that night at the Buck. Sarah had said everything he'd wanted to hear. He'd been elated, but also cautious. What if it had just been the booze talking?

What if it had been her loneliness or all the stress she was under? He hadn't wanted to hold her to it.

In the week that had followed, he'd tried to think of a way to approach her. At first, he'd thought he should have just told her how he felt. That they'd just met, and that he couldn't promise he loved her yet, but that he sure as heck didn't want to go away at the end of the summer. He'd wanted to talk with her, stone cold sober, about what was happening between them. But every time he had a chance, he froze, afraid that the truth wouldn't be what he wanted to hear. And every time he held back, he could see the wall around her grow a little taller.

That contract had been it—a gift from God, the perfect chance to tell her exactly how he felt. He may not have had a successful marriage, but he sure as hell had enough experience talking to women to know that sometimes the question wasn't the question. He'd read every word of that contract. He wouldn't let Sarah get herself into a tight spot.

But he still hadn't answered the question. Did he care what she did?

Will buried his face in his pillow, fighting the urge to yell. He'd tried to do the right thing. He couldn't tell her what to do. He didn't want to hold her back.

He cared. He cared a lot. But it didn't matter anymore. He had blown his chance.

Tossing off the covers, Will rolled onto his back, and Bart rested his head on his chest. He wished he could have a conversation with his dog. Maybe Bart would know what to do to fix this.

As he studied the ceiling, Will knew his own heart. He didn't want to go anywhere. He wanted to stay right here, even if it meant he never owned a business again. Will could see himself staying with Sarah through all the seasons, for years to come. It wasn't what he had always dreamed of, but dreams could change.

Would she believe him if he told her that his had?

Will reached for his phone, and the hair on the back of his neck stood up. Four missed calls from Rachel. No voicemails. No texts.

He tapped on her name, willing her to pick up. He'd talked to her as little as possible, lately, but he knew her well enough to know something wasn't right.

When she answered the phone, he didn't waste any time. "Is everything okay?"

She sniffed. "Never better."

"Rachel, what's going on?"

She sighed. "I'm here, Will. That's why I tried to call you."

He knit his brows together. What was she talking about? "Here?"

"In Alaska. Ketchikan, to be more precise. I hope I'm saying that right. This was the only flight I could get to your address, which, for your information, is in the middle of nowhere. The travel concierge I use had never heard of it."

Will sat up so suddenly that Bart scurried to the edge of the bed and jumped to the floor in annoyance. "You're what?"

"I'm here. I'll see you soon. The gentleman is loading my bags into his little plane now."

Will's stomach sank. Even from Ketchikan, he could see Mac grinning.

* * *

As soon as Rachel ended the call, Will sprang into action. With his heart in his throat, he pulled on clean clothes, and flew down the stairs. He grabbed the truck keys, breezing past Sarah on his way out the door. "Taking the truck to town. Be back soon."

If she replied anything, he didn't hear her. He was already in the cab, pulling out of the driveway the second the engine roared to life.

Will drove down the gravel road at record speed, bumping along so fast his head hit the ceiling of the cab. He reached up to rub the spot. A knot on his head was the cherry on top of this whole situation.

His shoulders sagged with relief when he saw he'd beaten Mac to the dock. It was short-lived as the faint hum of the float plane filled his ears.

He figured he'd stopped breathing at least three times while he waited for the plane to land. Rachel was chatty, and she couldn't have picked a more eager audience than Mac. The guy had been out to get him since day one, and he'd found the perfect partner-in-crime. How much had she told him?

The plane landed, and Will's whole body tightened as he watched them get out. One Italian leather boot attached to a shapely leg followed another. Rachel's hair hung in a chestnut curtain around her shoulders, not even a smudge to her garnet lipstick. Even in the least likely place on earth for her to show up, she looked like a movie star.

From the other side of the plane, Mac spotted him, greeting him with a smile and a wave. Will shivered as a sense of dread came over him.

Rachel ran over to wrap Will in a hug. It was more affection than she'd shown in the last few years of their marriage. "God, I am happy to see you. We have a lot to talk about."

He stiffened at her touch. "I think we have said everything."

She pulled back, lifting her sunglasses to peer at him. "Let's go back to the lodge where we can talk."

"Rachel, you can't go there."

She frowned, but her face remained smooth thanks to the

injections that Will had paid for. "Why not? Mac said it's the only place to stay on the island."

"Because you can't."

Will pressed his lips together. He didn't want to give her any details about Sarah. Rachel didn't need any more ammo.

"That's not a reason. I'm going, and we're talking." She spied the truck behind Will. "And you can drive me."

"You ready?" Mac asked, the smile stuck on his face.

She placed a hand on Will's arm. "I'm going to drive with my husband. Can you take my luggage there?"

Mac practically skipped to the driver's seat. "Absolutely."

"I'll be right back," Will told Rachel.

He jogged over to Mac. "Please don't say anything to Sarah."

Mac chuckled. "Oh, trust me, I don't need to say a word. You must think my sister is a real idiot if you believe I am all that stands between her and finding out the truth. You messed up."

Will clenched his fists, leaning closer. "I get you don't like me, but you realize she's going to be hurt?"

Mac's smile disappeared, and his voice turned quiet. "You don't know what hurt is. You don't know Sarah at all. If you think this will bring her down, you're underestimating her by a long shot. I'm just glad she's finding out about this before she wastes another minute. Hope you got a new job lined up."

With that, Mac put the truck in drive and pulled away, leaving Will to breathe a cloud of exhaust.

Left standing there with Rachel, it was almost laughable that only this morning, he thought he had ruined things with Sarah. This morning had nothing on this moment.

This time he had really, truly screwed up.

CHAPTER TWENTY-THREE

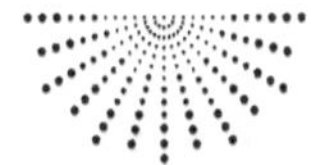

WILL

Will gripped the steering wheel, his heart heavy. The drive back to the lodge was both long and short. He wanted to get there as fast as possible so he could explain everything to Sarah. But then he remembered that the time to explain had come and gone, and that the only thing waiting for him was trouble.

As soon as he parked, Rachel flew out of the truck without so much as a glance back. Will heaved one foot and then another out of the cab, his walk back inside a death march compared to the vigor he'd left with. It occurred to him that in his panic, he hadn't even thought about Bart. Not that the little guy would have left Sarah's side.

His stomach twisted at the possibility that both he and Bart would leave this place sooner rather than later.

As he'd suspected, Will found Rachel talking to Sarah when he got inside. He searched Sarah's face for any signs of anger, or shock, or hurt, but she was the perfect hostess, her face a mask of patience.

"Of course, I understand. I'm so happy you could join us for the weekend," Sarah told Rachel. "Let's get you checked in."

Rachel's gaze connected with Will's. "It's fine. I'll stay with my husband."

She stepped close and snaked her arm around his, her touch unfamiliar.

He felt like he was choking, smothered by the past. He looked at Sarah again, but it was like she was made of stone.

"Bart! There you are!" His almost ex-wife called out. She knelt down. "Come to Mama!"

Bart sniffed the air and took a step back.

"Don't be shy." Rachel moved toward him.

Bart let out a low growl, and Will's mouth fell open. The dog had never been unfriendly to anyone, and especially not Rachel.

Rachel tried to keep a light tone, but he saw the annoyance flash in her eyes. "It's fine. He's just had too much time away from me, apparently. That's not happening again."

Will's stomach turned over. He didn't like the sound of that.

"You okay?" Sarah asked him. "You look a little pale."

He felt two inches tall. He had hurt her, and she was asking if he was okay.

"Fine," he mumbled.

Rachel headed towards the stairs, striding across the room like she owned the place. "Come on, babe. Grab my bags, will you?"

"Oh, Rachel," Sarah called out. "I don't know if you ate on the flight, but I was just about to fix myself some lunch. You two are welcome to join."

A grin spread across Rachel's face, the slow, confident smile of someone who was sure she had won. "We'd love to."

Will wanted to scream, to punch something. Instead, he

gathered up the two bulging suitcases and headed to the second floor.

As soon as he showed Rachel to his room, he shut the door behind himself and took a deep breath. "You can't stay here."

She laughed and waved him off. "It's a hotel, silly. That's what people do."

Will squared his shoulders. He always seemed to have to repeat himself with Rachel. She only heard what she wanted to hear. "No, you can't stay here. With me. In Alaska. You have a fiancé and a life back in Seattle. Oh, and how could I forget? A business. I don't know what you're doing, but this is legendary even for you. I'm your ex-husband, not a pawn you can use when you and Jason have a fight."

She sat on the edge of his bed, patting the spot next to her as she fluttered her eyelashes at him.

Will didn't move.

"Suit yourself." She crossed her legs with a sigh. "If you didn't want me to come find you, then why did you leave your address?"

This couldn't actually be happening. He ran his hand through his hair, certain he was in a nightmare. "Yeah, why did I do that? Probably because we just filed legal paperwork, and I wanted to make sure everything went through okay. As should you, you're the one who started proceedings. And cheated."

Rachel pouted. "Washington is a no-fault state."

He clenched his jaw. "I don't think that means what you think it means. You messed up, Rachel."

He said it for himself as much as for her. He had done the same thing, after all.

But then Rachel did something that shocked him. More than her cheating with his best friend, more than demanding his shares in the company. More than her showing up in Alaska.

She cried.

Fat tears rolled down her cheeks. "I know. I know I did."

Will's body tensed as he stared at her. He was only human. He'd never known what the hell to do when a woman cried, and certainly not when the woman was his ex-wife. "What's going on?"

She turned from him, covering her face with her hands. "It's not working out with Jason. When we were seeing each other when I was, um, with you." She sniffed. "It was different. But now we're trying to have this relationship, and it's awful. He's busy at work, and it's not fun anymore. We fight, the wedding plans are a mess. Nothing is ready."

Will resisted the urge to roll his eyes. Any shred of pity he'd felt shriveled up and disappeared. It shouldn't be a shock that Jason was busier at work now. Will had done more than anyone realized, and now they had to pick up the slack.

As far as their other relationship problems, that was life. Rachel didn't do hard stuff, never had. She only liked things that were easy, and fun, and pretty.

A knock came at the door, making both of them jump.

"Lunch is ready." Sarah's voice was muffled through the door.

"Be right there!" Rachel trilled, sounding totally at ease.

Will gaped at her. Rachel was either an A-list actress waiting to happen or a psychopath.

Maybe a little of both.

* * *

THERE WAS ONLY one good thing about lunch, and that was the fact that very few guests were around to witness the spectacle.

Will smiled as he took in the table. Sarah had outdone herself. Grilled salmon, garlic olive oil pasta, and a bottle of chilled white wine waited for them. If he didn't know better, he would have thought she was showing off.

"What are you so happy about?" Sarah muttered as she brushed past him.

Will cleared his throat and took a gulp of his wine. By the time he sat down, he had finished half the glass. He had a feeling he was going to need it.

Rachel didn't disappoint. Lunch consisted of her romanticizing their entire relationship, not once mentioning the part where she'd cheated and was currently engaged to someone else. Each lie from her mouth made his stomach twist up even tighter.

Will twirled pasta on his fork and forced himself to eat. Sarah had done an excellent job on the meal, but nothing would have tasted good to him right now. He wanted to sink into the floor.

"You've been together a long time," Sarah said.

Rachel reached for Will's hand, and her touch made him go cold. "Since high school. I can't imagine life without him."

Sarah looked at him, and he winced at the pain in her eyes. "Why did you come up here for the summer without your wife, Will?"

He reached for his wine with a shaky hand. There was no good way to answer that question. Because all the reasons he could come up with had the same problem—Will had had a wife back in Seattle, and he had kept that from Sarah.

"That was my fault," Rachel spoke for him. "I was too busy with the company, and Alaska had always been more of Will's dream. Turns out I couldn't live without him."

Sarah filled her glass with the last of the bottle. She set it back on the table with a thump. "Company?"

Rachel nodded. "The company we started. Will hasn't told you about it?"

Will gripped the seat of his chair with his free hand, the other resting limply under Rachel's manicured palm. *We*, she had said. Like she'd ever done anything other than spend the money he'd made. He'd lost track of the number of lies Rachel had told during the meal.

At least it couldn't get any worse.

Sarah raised an eyebrow. "No, he hasn't mentioned the company. Tell me more."

"Will, you're too modest," Rachel teased before turning her attention back to Sarah. "It's a multi-million dollar company."

"Is it?" Sarah's voice was flat as she reached for the bottle again. "I'll be right back. I need to get more wine."

When she left, he turned to whisper to Rachel. "You don't need to give her every detail of our lives."

Rachel laughed, and the sound made him cringe. "Who cares? It's not like you'll ever see her again."

His body grew numb as he realized that was the most likely outcome, and that he didn't like it one bit.

As he finished his meal in silence, he debated with himself. He couldn't decide who he was more disgusted with. Rachel for lying or himself for not telling the truth in the first place. The worst part was that everytime Will was about to get up the courage to unveil her little charade, Rachel opened her mouth to throw another shovelful of dirt on his grave.

After they'd eaten, Rachel claimed she was tired from the flight and went to lie down. Will jumped at the chance to talk to Sarah alone, and stayed behind to help her with the dishes. He desperately wanted to fix this, assuming it wasn't too late.

Sarah washed, and he dried without saying a word. He

held his breath as he watched her face for a sign, but she treated him with the same polite patience she'd displayed at lunch. It was one thing for Sarah to be pissed. Will would've understood that. Hell, he'd expected it. But to treat him like a stranger? That killed him.

Will hung up the dish towel and blurted out the words he had been wanting to say since he'd first spoken to Rachel on the phone today. "Sarah, I am sorry. I can explain everything."

She turned to look him in the eye. "Is that your wife?"

His stomach knotted up, but avoiding the truth was what had gotten him into this mess in the first place. "Technically…"

"And you really have a multi-million dollar company?"

Will ran his hand through his hair. This wasn't going well. Between this and lunch, maybe he'd be better off taking a vow of silence. And chastity. "I do, well I did, before…"

She held up her hand. "Then that's everything I need to know."

He felt light-headed as everything he cared about slipped away from him. He'd thought he would never feel this way about someone again. It had never occurred to him that he could lose everything just as quickly as it had come.

He reached for Sarah's hand, but she snatched it away, and he felt like all the air was sucked out of him. "Just tell me what to do. I'll do anything to make this right."

Sarah looked at him, her eyes glassy. "You think you're the only one with secrets? Well, you're wrong."

She pressed her lips together and turned her back on him as she walked to the office. Each passing second was measured by the sound of his own heartbeat in his ears. He waited for her to turn around. Waited for another chance. This time, he would plead his case.

But Sarah never looked back.

With a sinking sense of dread, Will watched her disappear into the office. She closed the door behind her, and with it, any chance for happiness Will had thought he'd had.

CHAPTER TWENTY-FOUR

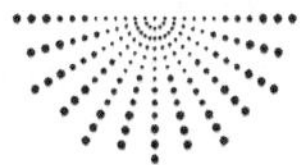

SARAH

Sarah had known pain. Having the love of her life disappear at sea and knowing she had done it had almost killed her. There had been so many nights in Los Angeles where she'd wanted nothing more than to come home, but she hadn't let herself. Watching people around her in LA move on with life, get married, and have kids while she stayed stuck in time had just plain sucked.

But none of that could match the pain of being only one room away from the man she'd thought she'd loved while he slept soundly with his wife.

Any suspicions she'd had about being an idiot had been confirmed.

Her own family had tricked her into coming back here.

She'd lost her job.

She'd told a married man she loved him and expected him to say it back. A married, millionaire man. Not the single handyman she had fallen for in the first place.

As if she'd needed a reminder that she was meant to go through life alone.

Sarah left a detailed note with everything Will needed to know for the next few days. She told Mac and her parents that she would be out of town. Mac offered to fly her out, but Sarah turned him down. She needed time to think, and the dark choppy water matched her mood. She stood on the deck of the ferry while the wind and salt battered her face, whipping away her silent tears.

An occasional wave of nausea swept through her, but she blamed it on her emotions and the aftermath of insomnia. Sarah had been on boats since she was a little girl. Never once had she suffered from seasickness.

The city of Ketchikan came into view, surrounded by the mega cruise ships docked there for the day. Sarah disembarked with heavy feet, going straight to the attorney's office. By virtue of being in Alaska, she'd been able to get an immediate appointment with the same law office her parents had used. It wasn't like the city had a huge clientele base.

Sarah handed the attorney her copy of the paperwork, covered in colorful sticky notes. "I need to make some changes."

The attorney peered at her through his glasses. "You're sure?"

She tucked her palms under her thighs, trying to drive the chill from her hands. "Certain."

"I can make the changes, but the other parties still have to sign."

She nodded. "That won't be a problem. I'm heading back on the ferry tomorrow. If it's not ready, can you send it to me?"

He glanced at his calendar. "It's pretty cut and dry. I can have it ready by morning."

Sarah let him know she'd be there when the office opened the next day. She didn't want to leave without the updated contract. The sooner this was done, the better. It was time to get back to real life. She only hoped her parents would understand.

With a deep sigh, Sarah stepped back out onto the street. She soaked in the rare sunshine as she made her way to the water. Looking over the harbor, Sarah tried to see it through Andre's eyes. She ached to understand him, as if maybe that would give her the answers she sought. Turning her back on the boats, she leaned against the railing, and pulled out her phone.

According to social media, the woman still lived in Ketchikan. She owned a bakery that sold those gourmet cupcakes that had become so popular.

Sarah had only met her once before, and she'd sworn she never wanted to see her again. Yet somehow, she found herself walking in the direction of the bakery in a daze, weaving through the throngs of cruise ship passengers browsing Alaska t-shirts and jade jewelry.

Slice of Heaven, the sign over the door read.

Her mouth twisted. How ironic when she had caused Sarah so much hell.

A bell chimed over the door as she walked in, and Sarah found herself unceremoniously face-to-face with the woman who had lived only in her nightmares for the past five years. "Julia?"

The woman grinned. "That's me. Do I know you? You look familiar. I'm sorry, I'm terrible at names."

Julia reached up to adjust her pink baseball cap embroidered with the bakery's name, and her hand glinted.

Married.

Sarah clenched her fist, digging her nails into her palm. She had come this far, after all. It was time to find out if the memories had been worse than the real thing. "We met once about five years ago."

The woman's smile faded as realization dawned on her. "Andre."

Sarah winced. Hearing his name out loud was like nails on a chalkboard. Sarah only ever spoke it in her head. "I'm sorry to bother you at work…"

"It's fine," Julia said, her smile back, though a little smaller. "I always wondered what happened to you."

Sarah knit her brows together. "To me?"

Julia nodded. "Yeah. I just remember meeting you that day, how upset you were. I don't know, I thought maybe you had suspected it. But you didn't. I wish I had never come."

Sarah's body slumped with exhaustion. She had spent so many sleepless nights over the years wondering what it would've been like, not knowing that Julia existed. But then she would have had only the guilt of sending Andre away, not the knowledge that he wasn't perfect to keep her from spinning off the planet.

Not that Sarah had told anyone, ever. Both secrets weighed her down. And the third secret, most of all.

She cleared her throat, her courage draining away. Sarah looked around the shop, taking in the bistro tables and thoughtful decorations. "This place is cute."

Julia crossed her arms with a smug look on her face. "Thanks. I make a fortune every summer. It's funny—my husband was worried about me opening up the place, and now I earn more than him."

Sarah felt light-headed. "Have you been married long?"

"Three years." Jula grinned as she waggled her hand, the diamond glinting. She touched her tummy. "Got a one-year-old too, and another on the way."

The walls closed in around her, and Sarah reminded herself to breathe. This woman had been the villain in

Sarah's nightmares for so long. Yet she had been thriving, while Sarah had barely been existing.

"Congratulations," Sarah whispered.

She was desperate to leave, but her feet were anchored to the floor. Sarah knew what five years of regret could do to a person. She couldn't change how things had gone with Andre, but she could leave things differently with Julia. "Look, I'm sorry if I was unfriendly that day. I was overwhelmed."

Julia gave her a sympathetic smile. "Don't be. I think you had it worse than me. I lost a boy, you lost a dream."

Sarah nodded, not trusting herself to speak.

Julia opened up the pastry case. "Let me give you a couple of things to take home. On the house. If you're ever in town, you know where to come for a cup of coffee and a chat."

Sarah accepted the pink box numbly and made her way to a park bench in the sun. When she opened the lid, she found four perfect cupcakes in different flavors.

She had expected to find a broken woman today, or at least an angry one. Sarah had spent every moment since Andre had disappeared hurt, angry, and scared. She still felt twenty-five and confused.

But Julia had moved on with her life.

Sarah spent the night in Ketchikan and collected the paperwork from the attorney on her way to the ferry.

Yesterday's sunshine was gone, leaving the usual gray skies. As the ferry eased itself into the open ocean, she watched the small city disappear behind her. The vessel gained speed, cutting and dipping through choppy water.

She'd thought she'd felt ill on the way here, but now her stomach twisted and her throat burned. It occurred to her that eating all four cupcakes in her hotel room last night in place of dinner had probably not been her best idea.

Stumbling to the bathroom, she got sick the minute the

toilet was in view. The flimsy stall door flung open, and she reached back to close it again.

"I've got that for you," a woman said behind her.

Sarah felt another wave of sickness coming and poised herself over the toilet. When she was done, the woman handed her a damp paper towel.

Sarah wiped her face, her throat burning. "Thank you."

"Feeling better?"

Sarah nodded and turned to an older woman smiling down at her with the patience only someone who had stood in her shoes could have.

"You look like you're about my daughter's age. She's going through the same thing right now. Not that I don't remember my own experience. I wasn't lucky enough to make it to the bathroom. Threw up on the side of the boat."

Sarah pushed herself up to stand and washed her hands. She wouldn't be eating cupcakes again for a while. "I think I'll be alright. Thank you."

"How far along are you?"

Sarah frowned. How far along? They'd just left Ketchikan. This woman should know as well as she did. "Um…."

The woman glanced at Sarah's midsection. "I am guessing the first trimester. That was my worst. You certainly don't have a giant belly yet!"

The nausea was replaced with dizziness, and Sarah was certain she was going to faint.

* * *

THE RIDE back to Darling was the longest of Sarah's life. She felt numb, and in her mind the same thoughts kept repeating themselves over and over. She couldn't be pregnant. It wasn't possible. She was careful. She took birth control.

In her mind's eye, she saw the dusty boxes of pregnancy

tests at the store in town, but that was asking for trouble. She would make an appointment to go back to Ketchikan in two weeks. She was past peeing on a stick—what she needed was a doctor.

She'd tried to do the math. It definitely, probably, most likely, she was almost sure, wasn't Aaron's. That was months ago, and she would've been showing by now.

That only left one possibility. Will.

The thought alone was enough to make her want to vomit again. A married man who'd lied to her face. She sure knew how to pick them.

But where had Will gotten protection from? Would he have needed those for his wife?

The dusty shelves at the store came back into her mind, and her body broke out in a nervous sweat as she realized they may have used an expired product. Now she was going to have a baby to show for it.

Her head tightened with a migraine. This couldn't be happening. Suddenly, her insistence on leaving this place and never looking back didn't seem so dramatic after all. No good came from being here.

She loved a man who was going to leave her. And she was pregnant. Again.

Sarah rested a hand on the outside of her jacket. Pregnant. She had told no one the last time. Only Andre. It had been the last thing she'd said to him before he'd gotten on the boat that had grown smaller and smaller until she couldn't see him anymore.

Then Julia had come to town, and not long after, Sarah had lost the baby. She had been hysterical, and no one had known why. No one had known that she'd lost the last connection she'd had to the love of her life.

Her parents had begged her to tell them what was wrong, but Sarah had kept her silence. She'd been embarrassed.

Andre had been cheating on her, and she'd been too devastated about the baby to say it out loud. So she'd left.

Sarah gripped the handrail as she walked off the boat. One thing at a time.

Right now, she had to face Will and Rachel. It was laughable that she might be pregnant with his baby, like something from a soap opera. Or it would've been laughable if she hadn't felt so completely confused about her own life.

CHAPTER TWENTY-FIVE

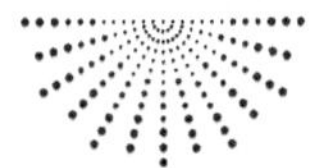

WILL

Will was driving himself crazy. Taking care of the lodge alone and getting Rachel to go home had been nothing compared to waiting for Sarah to get back. Every time the door had opened, he'd stopped breathing, hoping it would be her.

What if she didn't come back? Will dismissed the idea with a shake of his head. He wasn't thinking rationally. Sarah would be back, just like she'd said she would. People didn't just disappear.

She had been vague about her reasons for going to Ketchikan, and he hadn't pushed her. He was just happy she was still speaking to him at all. Then again, there weren't a lot of choices for a replacement who could run the lodge at the last minute. It wasn't like she'd fire him. Or would she?

He paced the living room, Bart at his heels. His body hummed with nervous energy, and he wished he could go for a hike, or maybe take Bart down to the water so the dog could run and snap at the foamy waves. But he'd promised

Sarah he would help at the lodge, so he'd kept himself stationed there in case a guest needed something. The last thing he wanted was for Sarah to come back and find him gone.

Bart soon tired of walking in circles and went to settle on his dog bed. Will envied him. In his next life, he wanted to come back as a dog. Dogs didn't have to worry about destroying their personal lives by being an idiot.

He made his way into the sitting room, where he eyed the liquor cabinet. His mouth watered. Was it too early for an Irish coffee? That might help him relax.

As he reached for the whiskey, the front door opened. His heart jumped into his throat. Was she back? He peered around the doorway.

Sarah walked in and slipped off her rain jacket and boots. She looked pale, her hair tangled. Dark smudges sat under both her eyes.

His heart squeezed. As miserable as he'd been, Sarah was the real victim here. And he was the one who hurt her. "How was the ferry?"

She avoided his gaze. "Same as always."

He decided not to beat around the bush. He didn't want to waste another minute of the limited time he had left with Sarah. "Rachel's gone."

Sarah's gaze flicked up. "Oh."

Will took a step towards her. He knew she was upset, and rightfully so, but once he left Alaska, he'd have no chance of fixing things between them. "Sarah, please let me explain. She didn't tell you the entire story."

She looked to the door of her office and then back at him. "Fine. Let's go sit down."

They made their way to the couch where Bart instantly hopped into Sarah's lap, positioning his head under her hand for pets.

Will cleared his throat. "Can I get you anything?"

She shook her head. "Just tell me what you want to tell me."

He took a deep breath. It was now or never. "Rachel and I haven't been romantic for a long time, okay? The marriage was basically over, or that's how it felt to me. Yes, I have a company with my best friend. Had. I had a company. He and I built it up from the time we were in college. I worked myself to the bone keeping up on everything in the office while Jason preferred to be out in the field. So maybe part of the problem was that I was almost never home."

His throat grew tight as he remembered his last few days in Seattle. "The night of our anniversary, Rachel comes and tells me she wants a divorce. Her and Jason, they've been seeing each other for a while."

Sarah frowned. "Your business partner? Your best friend?"

Will nodded. "And the best man at my wedding."

Her face fell. "Shit. That sucks."

"It gets better. As we leave the lawyer's office, Rachel hands me an invitation to their wedding. Not only was the ink not even dry on our divorce papers, our divorce wasn't even a thing when she started planning. Oh, and she took my shares in the company."

Sarah shook her head. "I don't understand. So why did she come here, claiming to be in love?"

Will ran a hand through his hair. "Because that's how she is. She uses people. If she isn't getting her way, she'll find a way. From the sound of it, running the company is a lot more work with me out of the picture. Now that she isn't just sneaking around with Jason anymore and they are in an actual relationship, it's apparently not all rainbows and sparkles."

"So you came up here to get away from all that? And you took this job because you needed it?"

He nodded. "Don't get me wrong. I have money, but it's tied up in retirement accounts and investments."

"Your home?"

"Sold it. Along with my truck. I had to. I couldn't count on income from the company anymore."

Sarah let out a deep sigh. "Have I said this sucks yet?"

Will chuckled. "I think it's worth saying more than once."

She looked at him, her eyes round with sympathy. "I'm sorry, Will. That sounds awful."

He reached for her hand, but it was limp and cold in his. "What I am saying is that I didn't mean to lie to you. I should've told you the truth. But I didn't expect this, us, to happen. I didn't even know how much it meant to me until Rachel showed up and it fell apart.

"But I'll be divorced soon, and there is absolutely nothing romantic going on between me and Rachel. By the time she left here, she was already back to talking about her wedding plans."

Sarah looked at her hand in his, then back up at him. "She is very beautiful."

"Until you get to know her." Will brushed the hair back from Sarah's face, and her expression softened. His heart soared as he realized he was getting through to her. "You're the most beautiful person in the world to me."

"Thank you," she whispered. "So, what's the plan now?"

He sat up, not sure what she was getting at. "What's the plan? The plan is this. I want to stay here, to be with you."

Sarah was silent for a moment. Will's heartbeat pounded in his ears, his confidence from a few seconds ago drained away, replaced by panic.

Her face was blank as she looked him in the eye. "I'm sorry, Will. That's not going to work. The thing is, I need to thank you, really. You helped me realize this isn't the life for me."

His heart crashed into the ground. "What are you talking about?"

She held his gaze. "I've accepted the job with Aaron."

His throat tightened. This wasn't happening. "But what about the lodge? Half of it is yours now."

Sarah gave a sad smile. "None of this is mine. I had the paperwork amended. It's all going to Mac."

Will swallowed. "That's why you went to Ketchikan."

She pulled her hand from his grasp. "So now that I'm leaving, and I am assuming you don't want to work for Mac, I think you need to consider other options."

Will searched her face. How had this gone so wrong? "You can't be serious. This is what you want? Really?"

She wrapped both hands around Bart, leaning over to place a kiss on his head. "It is." Her voice cracked.

Sarah gently lifted Bart and stood from the couch. She walked to the door before pausing. "It was good that Rachel came here. We were just fooling ourselves. We both know these kinds of things always come to an end."

She turned away, and he caught a glimpse of a tear running down her cheek. A cold dull pain seeped through his body as he felt the weight of the loss. The weight of everything that would never be.

CHAPTER TWENTY-SIX

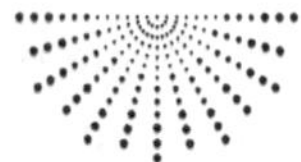

SARAH

Just like that, Will was gone. Sarah had expected him to fight, to resist, but he had done what she'd asked and left. She'd waited a full twenty minutes after she'd heard the door closing behind him to sob.

Pressing her face into her pillow, she hoped no one in the lodge could hear her.

She missed him intensely. She missed Bart's scruffy fur and Will's minty smell. The familiar loneliness came for her instantly, twirling its fingers in her hair and wrapping its icy hands around her heart.

Sarah knew she was the one who'd sent him away, and she knew it was the right thing to do. She didn't deserve to be in love, and look what had happened when she'd tempted fate? It would have never turned out well. That didn't mean that it felt good, once again watching the man she loved walk away from her. But Sarah had learned her lesson.

She passed the next week in a daze, a permanent smile frozen on her face. The show must go on. People paid good money for their stay at the lodge, and the last thing Sarah intended to do was shoot herself in the foot. The doctor had confirmed she was pregnant. Assuming she carried this baby to term, she wasn't going anywhere. The lodge had to stay in business.

That brought her to her next problem. She had to tell people. Her parents. Mac. Aaron. She couldn't take that job in Los Angeles, and she doubted Aaron's romantic interest would survive now that she was pregnant with another man's child. Even though she was scared, and she would love to run far away from Darling, it had helped nothing before. This time, she could not survive alone.

When the phone rang one morning, Sarah hadn't expected Natasha to be on the other end. She certainly hadn't expected her ex-boyfriend's mother to ask her out for lunch. Maybe because Sarah had no strength left, or maybe because she didn't trust herself to know when to be strong, she agreed. She was a fish in a tide pool, letting life move her.

Sarah went to the Buck, barefaced, with her hair up, and wearing a sweatshirt and jeans. She didn't see the point of trying anymore. Who was going to tell her differently, anyway? She had become as adept at dodging her parents as she had been all the way in Los Angeles, and Mac at least had enough common sense to avoid the hot mess she had become.

Sarah spotted Natasha right away, sitting alone in a booth by the window and clutching a coffee cup. The woman's eyes darted around, and she fidgeted in her seat.

With a deep breath, Sarah slid into the seat across from her. Why had Natasha asked her here? "I hope you haven't been waiting too long."

"Not at all. I'm glad you came." Natasha gave her a small smile. A tiny row of perfectly straight, white teeth showed themselves just for a second. Sarah sometimes forgot how delicate Natasha was. She didn't act like it.

Wolfie came over to take their order before leaving the two of them to sit in silence.

Sarah traced the nicks and dents on the table with her finger. "So why did you want to meet? Why now?"

Natasha sighed. "So we agree? It's easier if we just get to business?"

Sarah nodded. She was tired of pretending. She only had the energy for the truth.

Natasha took a deep breath. "I know about Julia. I know you know about Julia. How she is now."

Sarah stiffened in her seat. It wasn't possible. No one knew. That secret had weighed Sarah down for years. It was a burden she had carried alone. "What do you mean?"

Natasha broke her gaze, looking outside. "I will always love my son with a mother's love. Unconditional. Fierce. But he was a young boy, and even if he hadn't been, no soul in a human body with an ego does not make mistakes."

Sarah looked down at the table, her heart roaring in her ears. She willed herself not to be sick in the middle of the restaurant.

"I think he really loved you," Natasha continued. "But that's not the point. I can't prove that to you. The point is, you're not the one dead."

Sarah's head snapped up. Heat flared in her cheeks. "You wish I was the one who had died instead? Well, the joke is on you. I wish that too."

Wide eyed, Natasha reached out, wrapping her bony fingers around Sarah's hand.

"Not at all, my dear. I've never once wished that. And you shouldn't torture yourself with such thoughts either. Not when you have so much life ahead of you. So, why aren't you acting like it?"

Sarah swallowed. "How did you know?"

The older woman lifted her coffee cup with her free hand, taking a sip. "You know how."

Sarah nodded. Whether or not people believed Natasha, they all knew the stories. She knew things no one else did. "How much do you know?"

"I know you have a hole in your heart bigger than anyone knows about. So tell me. What happened? What happened, so that Julia makes hot pink cupcakes, and you're sitting here looking like walking death?"

Fat tears rolled down Sarah's face, leaving dark spots on her jeans. Just like Sarah's own mother would have, Natasha whipped a tissue out of her purse and handed it to Sarah.

"Thank you," Sarah mumbled. Her eyes burned as she struggled to regain her composure. "I don't know how to say this. I'm the reason Andre is gone."

Her voice cracked, and she pressed her lips together.

Natasha watched her carefully. "That's what you really think? Why?"

"Because that day, I told him I was pregnant." Sarah's heart slammed in her chest as she spoke the words out loud for the first time. "He was mad. He wasn't ready, I think. So when he left, and then Julia showed up, and he never came back, it was too much. I was devastated that he had cheated. Scared about losing the baby. Then destroyed when I lost the only connection to him I had left."

Natasha stood from her side of the booth and joined Sarah, wrapping her in a hug. Sarah winced at the touch. She didn't deserve compassion. "Oh, honey. You've been carrying that around this whole time? No wonder you haven't been able to move on, to be happy. None of that is your fault. My son made his choices, and that's our right when we are alive. Now it's your turn."

A bitter laugh escaped Sarah's throat. "If it's not my fault, then why did I do the same thing again?"

Natasha patted her back. "What do you mean, my dear?"

Sarah wiped her nose. "I'm pregnant again. Pregnant and alone. No one knows."

"But that's wonderful!"

"Wonderful?" The word caught in Sarah's throat. "It's terrifying. Everything is hopeless. I'm hopeless."

Natasha squeezed her shoulder. "Look around. This place is filled with people again. You see them walking outside. This town used to wheeze like a dying animal. Now it has the soft, slow breath of one growing in strength. You did this. You and Will."

Sarah's stomach sank. "Will left."

"What happened?"

"I sent him away. I… it's complicated." Sarah told Natasha the details, including Will's previous marriage and Rachel's surprise appearance in Darling.

"That doesn't have to be the end of the story."

Sarah sniffed. "Maybe not. But I'm not ready. I don't even know how to tell my parents, or Mac. Any of them."

Natasha nodded. "When you're ready, you'll know. But for now, let me say this. We don't always get to understand why everything happens in life. Don't get so busy searching for answers that time passes you by. Uncertainty is part of life. It's not a reason to stop living."

They grew quiet as Wolfie walked over. He dropped off their food without a word and hurried away as soon as the plates touched the table.

Sarah picked at a French fry, but her appetite was gone. Maybe Natasha was right. Sarah had wasted years, desperate for a reason for why everything had happened. But knowing the reason wouldn't change the past. "I can't get that time back."

Natasha smiled at her. "That's the whole point. You're not supposed to be looking back."

* * *

SARAH'S unplanned meeting with Natasha had been exactly what she needed. Like the late morning sun burning off the marine layer, Sarah could see clearly what she had to do next.

She turned down the job offer from Aaron. She hadn't planned on telling anyone about her pregnancy yet, but suddenly she didn't care. After he pushed for the third time about why she was passing on his offer, she told him about her condition. He quickly accepted her decision after that.

She'd thought she'd feel sad to lose the last connection she'd had to her life in California, but she was surprised to find that she felt relieved instead. She had spent the past five years running from the past—now she was planning for the future.

Next, Sarah told her parents and Mac she wanted to stay in Alaska. Her change of heart shocked them, to say the least.

Her mom gaped at her. "You want to stay here and run the lodge? You're not doing it just to make us happy?"

Sarah nodded. She wanted to tell them everything, but she wasn't ready. She needed more time. "Yes, I think it's best. There's really nothing for me in California. At least here I have family."

Her mom stood and wrapped Sarah in a hug. "Oh honey, I'm so glad to hear that."

Her dad smiled. "We'll make it nice for you. We can fix up your room however you want."

Only Mac stayed silent, sizing her up from across the room.

Later that night, after everyone left, a knock came at the

door. For a few self-indulgent seconds, Sarah let herself believe it could be Will.

She was more surprised than disappointed to see Mac standing there instead. "Did you, by chance, hit your head? We just said goodbye like an hour ago."

He scratched his beard. "Interesting question. Why don't I ask you the same thing? Because it wasn't too long ago, you couldn't wait to watch this place disappear in the rear-view mirror and never see it again."

Sarah crossed her arms. "I don't know what to tell you, Mac. People change their minds. Welcome to being human."

Mac pushed past her into the living room to fix himself a whiskey. "I actually think you know what to say. And now that I've waited long enough in my truck down the road, mom and dad should be well in bed. Meaning you have an audience of one."

"For what?"

"For the truth, dummy. What's really going on?"

Sarah reached up to massage her forehead. "Why can't you just accept that I'm staying?"

"Because even though we don't always, or almost never, get along, and I haven't seen your face in five years, I know you." He held the glass of whiskey out to her. "Would a little of this help?"

Sarah reached for it, and then she dropped her hand. "No, thanks."

He cocked his head to the side. "You got plans tomorrow?"

Sarah hesitated, and Mac's eyes grew wide. "Son of a gun. Are you pregnant?"

She crossed her hands over her stomach. "Why would you ask that?"

Mac held her gaze. "Are you?"

Sarah took a deep breath as she tried to stay calm. The

last thing she needed was for a guest to stumble downstairs, woken mid-slumber by her flipping out. "Please don't tell Mom and Dad."

Mac laughed. "You don't think they'll notice?"

"I don't know how to tell them yet. I don't... not a lot of people know."

Her brother covered his face with his hand. "Oh God, it's Will's isn't it. What a piece of shit."

"There's a bit more to the story than you know. They were practically divorced—"

Mac cut her off. "Congratulations. Wish I could say I'm happy for both of you, but it looks like only one of you is standing here. You're not alone. At least you have us."

He slammed the glass down on the coffee table and walked towards the front door.

"Mac, please, don't say anything. To anyone," she begged.

He snorted. "You know me. I don't like other people in my business, and I return the favor."

The door slammed behind him, and Sarah cringed. At least, Mac wouldn't be able to blame her for not taking any real responsibility this time. Because this time, she would stay, even when it seemed so much easier to leave.

CHAPTER TWENTY-SEVEN

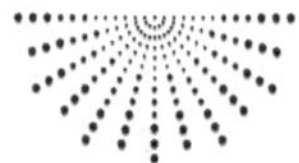

WILL

Will glanced at his reflection and reached for the comb again. It seemed every time he looked in the mirror, his hair stood on end. But then he hadn't been able to go even five minutes without running his hand through his hair. Maybe if he taped his arms to his sides.

Bart looked up, let out a sigh, and flopped to the ground. Will agreed. This whole evening was better off forgotten.

Will didn't know what had possessed him to agree to go to Rachel's wedding. Maybe a small part of him didn't believe it would actually happen. Maybe he needed something, anything, to take his mind off Sarah and everything he'd left behind on that island. Maybe he just needed five minutes where he could forget that he was totally and completely heartbroken.

Not that he didn't have plenty to do. He didn't want to live in the extended stay hotel room forever. The cheap carpet and tiny kitchenette were a stark contrast to the cozy lodge.

It had taken Will no time at all to return to skipping most meals and picking up fast food when he did eat. The most he managed to make at home these days was black coffee. As Will sipped the bitter brew, his mind would wander to that first morning when Sarah had cooked them breakfast. He smiled at the memory of her fixing a piece of bacon for Bart. Even though Will had felt only half-alive that day, hungover and miserable as he'd been, he'd still felt better than he did right now.

Finding a job was another item on his to-do list. He was burning through his savings faster than he'd realized. In Alaska, he'd had almost no expenses since his room and board had been part of the deal. Not to mention that Seattle wasn't known for being a budget-friendly city—even his bare bones set up cost him dearly.

Will could have had a job by now. He had hundreds of contacts in the industry, people who would've happily swooped up someone with his skill and experience. But he wasn't ready to deal with the questions about his old company, or his ex-wife. Even if no one he'd talked to so far had brought it up, they'd looked at him with enough pity to make him consider unemployment.

He did have a small safety net. The modest salary Sarah had paid him over the summer sat in a tidy pile of uncashed checks in the bottom dresser drawer. But Will would rather pay penalties for withdrawing from his retirement accounts early than cash a single one. He knew there was no hope of fixing things with Sarah, but cashing those checks would wipe away the last shred of romance. The last thing he wanted was for Sarah to think their time together had been nothing but a business transaction to him.

He ran the comb through his hair yet again and glanced at his watch, his stomach sinking. He'd dragged his feet long enough. It was time to go.

The ceremony was across town, and since he was getting there with public transportation, he needed to leave now. Will had just reached for his coat when a knock boomed at the front door. He almost jumped out of his skin, the sound larger-than-life in the quiet hotel. Bart whimpered and crawled under the bed. Will considered joining his dog, but instead he looked through the peephole. His eyebrows shot up as he looked at the last person on earth he'd expect to show up here.

The door boomed again, making Will's head vibrate. He took a deep breath, not ready to open the door yet. "Who is it?"

"You know who it is, city slicker."

Will cringed and undid the lock. "Hey Mac."

Mac dismissed Will with a wave of his hand. "Don't worry about being nice. That's not going to do much at this point. Can you guess why I'm here?"

"I'm guessing not because I left my sunglasses on your plane?"

"You're smarter than you look," Mac said, kneeling down to scratch Bart's ears. The little dog had emerged at the sound of the familiar voice. The giant seemed to have a soft spot for the dog, and Bart showed him his belly like a traitor.

Will checked the time again, clearing his throat. As much as he didn't want to go to this wedding, he wanted to be stuck in the tiny room with Mac even less. "I really need to get going."

Mac straightened to face him, his green eyes unblinking. "Right. I just need to know something. Why did you leave?"

Will clenched his fists. Mac was the last person he wanted to discuss this with. "Sarah told me to. Look, I offered to stay, to make things work. But she made it clear that me staying in Darling wasn't an option."

Mac rolled his eyes. "You have no mind of your own?"

Will's face grew hot. It wasn't enough that he'd had his heart ripped out of his chest? Now he had to take crap from Mac? "I don't know what to tell you. I tried, okay? I tried when Rachel was there. I tried when Rachel left. Sarah wanted me gone."

"Do you want to be there?"

Will's anger melted away, replaced by the pain of wanting something he couldn't have. "Of course. I want to be there more than anything. Nothing feels right since I left. But it doesn't matter. Sarah went back to LA, right?"

He watched Mac move across the living room to peer out the window. "Crappy view," he said, ignoring Will's question.

Will rubbed his forehead. He and Mac weren't exactly on friendly terms, and this entire conversation was weirding him out. Heck, Mac's presence in Seattle was bizarre in itself. "What are you doing in Seattle, anyway?"

Mac lifted a shoulder. "Apparently, I'm the only one with emotional intelligence around here. Someone had to do something."

Will choked on a laugh. "Thanks, but I have to get going. I'm going to be late."

Mac cocked an eyebrow. "To what?"

Will hesitated. He knew Mac wasn't going to like his answer, but it probably couldn't make things any worse. "Rachel's wedding."

Mac looked like he was going to be sick. "God, you're an idiot."

He stepped out the front door, but not before leaving Will with one last thought. "It's not just about you and Sarah."

Will watched him go, wondering for the first time how Mac had gotten his address. Then moving found its way to the top of Will's priorities. He grabbed his jacket and stepped outside. He walked halfway down the hall before turning back to double check that he'd locked the door, just in case

Mac decided he had more to say. Will had had enough surprises for one day.

* * *

THE WEDDING at the beautiful church was to be followed by a reception at a restaurant with a view of the city. A stretch limo of a German make was waiting in the church parking lot, and just inside the front door, stood a table of small gift bags. Will nabbed one only to find artisan chocolates and crystal wine stoppers etched with the wedding date inside. A glance at the crowd told him that at least two hundred people had shown up, and that was a conservative estimate. As usual, his ex-wife had spared no expense.

Knowing how much things could cost in Seattle, his head hurt when he tried to imagine what the final tally for the event would be. Thank God, he wasn't paying the bill. That was Jason's problem now.

Will took a deep breath, and the smell of fresh-cut flowers filled his nose.

The best part about today was that he could truly call Rachel his ex-wife. Their divorce was finalized, and her marriage to a new man was about to begin. Any ties to Rachel and Will's old life lived only in the history books. It felt like his special day just as much as Rachel's.

The worst part was that it meant nothing without Sarah. He was free to be with the woman he loved, but she didn't want anything to do with him.

Will tried to keep a clear head as he made his way to a seat. Naturally, he and Rachel had mutual friends, and almost all of them were in attendance. They all greeted him with the same mix of curiosity and sympathy.

They had it all wrong. He had been upset when he'd first found out about Rachel and Jason, but now he only felt relief.

Not that this was the day to explain his side of the story to anyone. Despite what his ex-wife thought, Will wasn't a monster. He wasn't going to make Rachel out to be one on her wedding day, either.

As Will scoped out a seat towards the back, he felt a tap on his shoulder.

He turned to find Ally, one of Rachel's close friends. Ally blinked her giant blue eyes framed by false lashes. "Rachel needs you."

Will didn't move. The crowd had taken their seats, and he had no plans to inadvertently become part of the wedding procession. "The ceremony is about to start. Wouldn't she prefer to talk after her wedding? She is kind of the main character."

Ally frowned, or Will assumed she was trying to. Her lips puckered out, but years of injections left the rest of her face unchanging. "She said now."

Will gave up and followed Ally to the bridal suite, a familiar tight feeling creeping up his back. He reminded himself that he and Rachel weren't married anymore. He was getting worked up over something that didn't concern him.

Ally ushered him into the room. When the door closed behind him with a soft click, it was just him and Rachel in the room.

He stared at his ex-wife's back as she sat at the vanity. "What did you want, Rachel?"

She let out a sob, and his stomach sank. He took a tentative step towards her. "What's wrong?"

The question only made her cry harder.

Against his better judgment, Will went to kneel beside her, opting for silence this time. His strategy had shifted from fixing the problem to at least not making it worse. Clearly, he still knew next to nothing about women.

"Am I making a huge mistake?" she squeaked between sobs.

Will took a deep breath. He had seen Rachel cry more in the past month than he had in their entire marriage. She had once held back tears when she'd broken her ankle, just because she didn't want to mess up her makeup. "With what?"

"This wedding."

"If you love Jason and…"

Her wails grew louder, and Will's sympathy turned into frustration. "Rachel, I don't know what to tell you."

"Do you still love me?" she whispered.

He jumped to his feet. He couldn't have been more shocked if she'd reached out and slapped him. "I know you aren't serious right now. Jason is standing out there. Hundreds of people are here for your wedding."

She looked up at him, her light blue eyes pleading. "But I think I still might love you."

Will took a step back. "It's just wedding stress or something, I don't know. But it's not love. Love isn't cheating, betrayal, or lies. Love is doing whatever you can to show the other person you care, even if it hurts you."

His throat grew tight. Suddenly, he didn't know why he was standing there staring at his ex-wife in a wedding dress when he should be on an island in Alaska.

Plus, he needed to know what Mac had meant when he'd said it wasn't just about Will and Sarah.

There was only one way to find out.

He leaned over and gave Rachel a hug and a kiss on the cheek. "You'll be okay. You always land on your feet."

She reached for him, parting her lips just as he pulled away.

He heard her calling his name, demanding to know where

he was going, but he didn't look back. He just kept walking, away from the old and towards the new.

* * *

WILL TOOK the stairs two at a time, his lungs burning. All that mattered was getting back to his apartment as fast as possible.

He took his keys out of his pocket, but when he looked up, they hit the floor with a crash. "Mac? What are you still doing here?"

Mac lifted himself from where he sat on the floor. "Hoping you weren't as stupid as you looked."

"What does that mean?"

"It means you better be back here because you're packing for a trip to Alaska."

Maybe it was a stupid thing to do. Maybe Sarah was already back in LA. But the ache of missing her, of wondering if he'd made a huge mistake, overpowered his doubts. "I have to."

Mac gave a nod. "Damn straight. Now pack fast. I'll take the dog out."

Will peered at him. "Why are you helping me?"

Mac rolled his eyes. "Don't flatter yourself. I'm helping my sister. Besides, I would hate to waste this extra ticket I have to Ketchikan, where my plane is waiting. I'll let you connect the dots. Try not to take too long."

Will tilted his head to the side. "You knew I would come back."

Mac lifted a shoulder. "I had nothing to lose. Either you come back, and I'm the hero. Or you don't, and I know once and for all you're a piece of shit. Regardless, I can sleep at night."

Will raised an eyebrow.

Mac curled his lip in a snarl. "Don't make this out to be a touchy feely moment. Have you ever been around a woman with a broken heart? I can't stand it another day. I don't know why any man ever gets involved. Seems like a surefire way to be miserable. Now, are you just gonna stand there, or can we leave?"

Will unlocked the door to his apartment, the keys shaking in his hand. He was doing this. He was going to run after something he wanted, even if there was no guarantee he'd get it in the end. Because if he didn't, the only guarantee was that Sarah would be gone from his life forever.

Bart shot out the front door and yipped as Mac picked him up.

"Are you sure you don't like dogs? Because he seems to like you."

Mac huffed. "He isn't a dog. He's a rat."

But as Mac and Bart headed downstairs, Will heard the giant cooing under his breath.

Not for the first time that summer, Will wondered if he knew anything at all. He shook his head. There would be time to think later. Right now, he had to pack.

Luckily, he'd already gotten rid of most of his stuff. Selling the condo had meant thinning out a lot of his possessions, and the move into the extended stay pet friendly hotel suite had gotten rid of the rest.

He grabbed a suitcase and began tossing in the same clothes he'd had with him this summer.

Then he paused. It wasn't summer anymore.

He did a quick search on his phone of what weather he could expect waiting for him in Alaska.

He shivered at the results, grabbed his warmest jacket from the closet, and knew he would still have to beg Mac to pick him up something in Ketchikan down the line.

That was if Sarah wanted him in Alaska at all. What if she

told him to get lost again? Will pushed the thought to the back of his mind. He only needed one focus right now—seeing Sarah in person so he could apologize. His heart might stay broken, but at least he would have the peace of mind of knowing he'd done every damn thing he could.

He zipped up the suitcase and slipped his laptop into his backpack. It was now or never.

Bart and Mac returned, and the scruffy dog happily hopped into the carrier.

Will picked up the suitcase. "Ready?"

Mac turned his back to Will and headed downstairs. "I hope you don't plan on talking this much the whole trip."

CHAPTER TWENTY-EIGHT

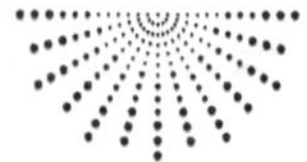

WILL

Will wasn't delusional. He knew he wasn't the smartest guy on the planet, but he at least liked to think he was mildly intelligent. He'd built a million dollar business after all. He'd kept himself and his dog alive. For a while, he'd even thought he'd had a successful marriage.

But when he saw Sarah sitting at the end of the dock, he realized that he knew nothing at all. Nothing that could prepare him for this moment at least.

Her back was turned to him, and he could only see her auburn hair and black puffy jacket from where he was standing.

It was quiet out here now, almost like it had been at the beginning of his stay. During the summer it had seemed like the island was reawakening; the light lasting longer every day, berry bushes bursting with color, tourists coming and going.

Now Darling felt heavy and somber, as if the island was stuck in that weird place between being awake and asleep.

The sky was more gloomy, the clouds dark and thick. The water seemed to have turned from blue to black. A chill in the air left his throat cold.

It was perfect. The view was more beautiful than the wedding chapel in Seattle, and Sarah more beautiful than any bride he'd ever seen.

He let Bart out of the carrier, and the small dog immediately trotted over to Sarah. Will followed behind, careful to step lightly on the wooden dock.

Bart nuzzled Sarah's side, and she turned to look at the dog, her eyebrows high on her forehead.

Will sucked in his breath. She was the most beautiful, incredible person in the entire world. And he was an idiot.

Her eyes grew large when she saw his face. She scrambled to stand. "Will. What are you doing here?"

Will knew he'd caught her off guard by showing up like this, but he was thankful she was at least talking to him. When he'd left, her demeanor towards him had been cool and professional, as if any familiarity had been sucked out of their relationship. It had hurt more than she could know, and Will had dreaded the possibility of it being the same way when he returned.

Even if Sarah didn't want anything to do with him, coming back had been the right thing to do. Will had caused the one person he cared the most about in the world a lot of pain, and it killed him. Even if he couldn't change what had happened, he could at least give her some answers.

The apology tumbled out of him, pushed to the surface by the regret he'd felt since the moment he'd left Darling. "I'm an idiot. I should've fought. I should've stayed. I should've told you the truth the moment I met you. Because that's when I knew I loved you."

Her eyes grew watery, and his heart squeezed. How could he have caused the woman he loved so much suffering?

"Leaving was the right thing to do. There's nothing for you here. You wouldn't be happy. When winter comes and it's mostly dark, and you can't do anything, you'll hate it. You had a career, Will. A business. You think you can do that here?"

He took a step towards her. He'd had all the same thoughts. And had come to the conclusion that none of it really mattered, not as much as being with Sarah. "What makes you think I want to do that at all?"

She wiped at her cheeks. "What do you want, then?"

Will placed his hands on her shoulders, looking her in the eye. "You. I want you. What do you want?"

She held his gaze. He held his breath as he prayed this wouldn't be the last time he held her in his arms. Finally, she spoke, her voice soft. "I want you, too."

Will pulled her to him and lowered his head, knowing he would remember this kiss for the rest of his life.

She grew soft in his arms, melting into him, and he knew then he would never leave Alaska. Because he never wanted to leave this spot, this moment.

She pulled back, and Will's eyes flew open. "What's wrong?"

Sarah looked away. "I want you to stay."

Coldness seeped into his belly. "But. It sounds like there's a but."

She reached down to pick up Bart, as if holding him made her feel safe. "But you need to know everything."

Will gave her arm a reassuring squeeze. "Sarah, there is nothing that can change my mind. I want to be with you. I know we only just met, so I am not saying that you have to promise me right now it's forever. But can we at least give it a shot?"

He swallowed, determined to plead his case. "I was with someone almost my whole life, and in the end, it was a mess.

I don't know how long things were bad, and I think that right there tells you everything you need to know. I didn't even notice when the love was gone. So even though logically I know we should play it safe, well, you can still get hurt."

Her eyes filled with tears. "Oh, Will. That's not the problem. I want to be with you. But I don't know if you want to be with me. I am afraid I'll hurt you."

Will knit his brows together. "What are you talking about?"

"I told you about my ex-boyfriend before. About Andre." Her voice grew small. "What you don't know is that I killed him."

CHAPTER TWENTY-NINE

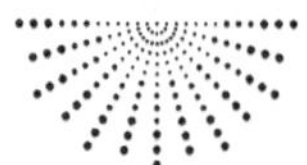

SARAH

"Sarah, what are you saying?" Will asked, his face a shade paler than before.

She swallowed. She felt like she'd drank handfuls of water from the sea, growing only more thirsty. It felt the same as wanting love and having none.

"Andre and I, things weren't perfect. I know you can understand when I say this, but I thought they were. I thought we were in love. I never wanted to leave this place, not unless he came with me. All I cared about was being with him."

A rare gust of wind blew past them, and Bart shoved his snout into the crook of her arm. It should've warmed her heart, but it made it crack a little more. It was just one more thing she would miss. She considered reaching for her words, taking them back. But Will deserved more than that.

"Maybe it was young love. Maybe things would've ended, naturally, if they hadn't ended the way they did." She gave him a small smile as she thought of the good times with Andre.

Will stayed silent, allowing her the space to talk.

"Almost no one knows. At the time, not a single person did. But I was pregnant."

She watched Will's face carefully, but it remained neutral. "Pregnant, scared, and excited. I told Andre that day, and, well, I don't know. I guess I thought he would be happy. I thought maybe he would ask me to marry him. We had talked about it, you know. We weren't teenagers anymore. He and I had been together for years at that point.

"But he got mad. He started yelling, saying I did it on purpose to trap him here. Saying he didn't think it was true. He asked me who else I had slept with."

A shiver ran down Sarah's spine. She had never felt so small as she had that day. It had been like waking up to a morning of sunshine, and then having a storm roll in and slap her face with sheets of rain.

"Sarah, I'm so sorry," Will whispered.

She gave a shake of her head. "Don't be. I shouldn't have told him then. It was the last catch of the season. He was tired. It wasn't the right time. I begged him to stay, to talk to me, but like everyone else on this damn island, he needed every dollar. So he got on the boat and sailed away."

Sarah could see it perfectly in her mind's eye, his blue jacket bobbing, growing smaller and smaller. She'd stayed there until there was nothing at all to see. She hadn't known then it would be the last time she saw him.

"They looked for him, of course." She gestured out to the water. "But you've seen this place, seen it from the air. It would be easy to disappear, whether or not you did it on purpose.

"So here I am, alone and pregnant and no one knows, living with the fact that I chased him away from shore that day. Then if you can believe it, it gets worse. Some girl shows up from Ketchikan to talk to me, and it turns out they were hooking up."

"That's why he asked you who else you'd slept with."

Sarah gave a curt nod. "Because that's exactly what he was doing."

Will took a step towards her, as cautious as if she were a wild animal. "You have to know you have nothing to feel guilty for."

"I wish it were as easy as believing that," she whispered.

"And the baby?"

She swallowed, wondering if she would ever reach a point where thinking about that memory didn't hurt. "Miscarriage."

His face fell. "Oh, God. Sarah, I am so, so sorry."

She willed her voice to stay steady. "I went to visit her, you know. That girl from Ketchikan. She's married now, a mom, and she has her own business. She went on living. I sometimes feel like I died with Andre that day."

"That is a horrible burden to carry. But Sarah, you have to know it's not true. And if you can't believe that right now, then know that I won't leave you."

She looked at him, the cold Alaskan air steeling her nerves. "Not even if I told you I was pregnant?"

"Not even if you told me that." He smiled.

"This isn't theoretical, Will."

The look on his face told her everything she needed to know.

Will Brooks did not, could not, love her. He would leave Alaska again, and he wouldn't come back.

She could feel her heart cracking, shattering into a thousand pieces.

Then he was wrapping her in a hug so tight that Bart squeaked.

"I've never loved you more," he whispered into her hair, his breath tickling her ear and warming her heart.

The sense of relief she felt was followed by slow, rolling tears that landed on Will's jacket. "What do we do now?"

"I don't care," he said. "Whatever you want. I just want to be with you every summer. For fifty more summers. For however long we have."

Suddenly, it felt as if a load had been lifted from her shoulders. Maybe having all the answers, understanding why everything had happened the way it had, wasn't as important as what was happening right now.

Her memories of Andre and the baby she'd lost would always stay with her. But at what cost? For so long, she'd sacrificed the present to atone for the past.

She would never have all the answers. But what she did have was a man by her side who loved her completely, loved her even though he knew the darkness in her heart.

Sarah took a deep breath. She couldn't change the past. But she could change her future.

EPILOGUE

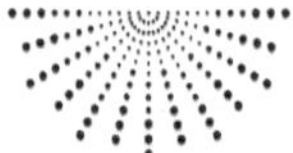

SARAH

Sarah wondered if she would ever get used to Will being back. The first morning they woke up together, she reached out for him only to find cool bed sheets. In a panic, she ran downstairs in her pajamas to find him measuring the oven.

She gasped as she tried to catch her breath. "What are you doing?"

"Good morning, beautiful." He grinned. "I'm ordering you a new oven."

Sarah shook her head. "One, I can't let you spend the money on that. Two, you're not the handyman anymore."

"One, I want to," he countered. "Two, I want to."

He reached for her, nuzzling her neck, and goosebumps rose on her arms as a tingle traveled to her toes. "Let me take care of you."

She tipped her head back, her body warming at his touch. "Then come take care of me upstairs."

"With pleasure." He swept her up. "Gotta do this while I can."

She laughed as they made their way back to the bedroom in the suite they'd moved into together. They didn't have anything to hide anymore, after all.

If anyone had any comments about Will's return, they'd kept them to themselves. Wolfie had greeted him with a smile and a beer. Sarah's parents had come over for dinner and acted like he'd never left, and Vivian filled his orders at the store without questions. Maybe they were being polite. Or maybe they'd known he would come back.

Sarah and Will made plans to run the lodge together the next summer, and Will continued to make improvements—including installing a new state-of-the-art oven that actually made Sarah not hate cooking so much.

Before they knew it, it was time. Heavy coats and baggy clothing could only hide so much.

Sarah looked at Will, and he squeezed her hand. "Are you ready for this?"

She smiled as a sense of certainty settled over her. She wasn't alone. They would do this together. "Absolutely."

They went downstairs and joined the family in the dining room.

Her mom already sat at the table with a glass of wine. Her dad was carrying the salad in from the kitchen, followed by Mac who was holding the main course.

"Would you like a glass, darling?" Her mom asked, her rosy cheeks a clear sign that she was enjoying her full mobility again, including access to the wine rack.

Sarah shook her head and looked at Will one more time.

He gave a nod. "Tell them."

She took a deep breath. She could do this. "Actually, I won't be able to have wine for a while. Or schnapps. Or Wolfie's beer. Because I'm pregnant."

Her mom shrieked and stood up as quickly as she could.

Sarah left Will's side to meet her halfway. "Darling, I'm so happy for you. A baby."

Her dad came over and set a hand on Sarah's shoulder, his eyes watery. "My little girl is all grown up."

The butterflies in her stomach transformed into a gushy, warm feeling. She was going to be a mom. She was home. She wasn't doing this alone. "Thank you."

Everyone turned to Mac, who broke his silence. "What? I'm happy for you, if this is what you want."

"Maverick Carter," his mom chided him.

"Jesus Christ." He ran his hand through his hair. "I'm happy for you, okay. I've always thought I'd be a good uncle. Just didn't imagine this city slicker would be the dad."

"That's why we need you," Sarah said. "God forbid the kid be a city slicker, too."

Mac's mouth quirked. "Damn straight."

Her mom clasped her hands together. "I want to hear everything. When are you due?"

"Early spring."

"Are you going to keep living at the lodge?" her mom asked, her face hopeful.

Sarah laughed. "What you're really asking is if we're going to get married."

Her mom blushed. "I've been wondering, but you know we aren't stuffy. We will love you all the same."

"Allow me to settle any doubts." Will turned to her father. "Do I have your permission?"

Her dad grinned. "You've had it for a long time."

Will pushed back his chair and got down on one knee. Sarah gasped, the butterflies returning. They had discussed having a civil ceremony, but nothing fancy.

"I want you to have a real proposal," Will said, as if he'd read her mind, something he seemed to do more and more lately. "I love you. There's nothing more important to me than being here with you and our child. The only thing more perfect would be calling you my wife."

He opened up a small ring box, and through her tears, Sarah saw a lone emerald-cut diamond on a gold band. It was simple and timeless, just like this place. Just like her love for Will.

She placed her hand on her chest, certain it was going to burst. "Are you sure you want to do this again? Get married again?"

Mac slammed his hand down on the table. "You're supposed to say yes, dammit!"

"Yes," Sarah said, and her family burst into cheers.

Her mom pointed to the kitchen. "Richard, get me the calendar. We have a wedding to plan."

Her dad's chair scraped back as he immediately stood to do his wife's bidding.

Sarah looked up to see Mac staring at her. "What is it?"

He raised an eyebrow. "I'm just glad it's you and not me."

She smiled. "How funny. Because I was just thinking that it's your turn."

He rolled his eyes as he finished his beer. At least some things never changed—it was almost comforting how she could count on Mac to always be the same.

Her mom held up the calendar. "Okay honey, so right now, we have a little time until summer, and you know what gorgeous weather we have in summer."

Seeing the calendar in her mom's hand made Sarah's chest expand as she thought about everything that had happened in those pages. She had started this year alone, far away, and with the weight of the world on her shoulders. Now she was pregnant again. In love again. Happier than she'd ever been.

One day, she would tell her parents everything, the whole story. But for now, there was only one story she cared about. The one she was living now.

A NOTE FROM THE AUTHOR

Thank you for taking the time to read my book. I hope you had as much fun reading it as I did writing it.

If you did enjoy it, and want to help other people discover Sarah and Will's story, please consider leaving a review at the retailer where you purchased this book. It would absolutely make my day (especially if share who your favorite character is!).

Thank you kindly.

<h1 style="text-align:center">ACKNOWLEDGMENTS</h1>

This is always the hardest part of the book to write. How can I possibly thank everyone? How can I put into words how grateful I am? But I will try.

To Austin, who really brought out the magic in the story. Thank you for your notes, your help, and your encouragement.

To the team at Best Page Forward, for creating both gorgeous visual art and gorgeous word art. I love it!

To Sarra, who I am so excited to share this story with. After years of dreaming about this moment, here it is!

To my mom, who has always been there for me. Thank you.

To Papa, for telling me I was capable, even though I didn't know of what. Now I do. I was capable of this. I was capable of dreaming.

Thank you all.

ABOUT THE AUTHOR

Lark Holiday is the author of feel-good and funny romances. She lives in California with her opinionated dogs and her human family. When she's not writing, she spends her time going for walks, vacuuming dog hair, and feeling like she should probably be writing.

Though Lark is based in California now, she lived in Alaska many times over the past few decades. Her time in The Last Frontier inspired the Darling Men series.